CHOICES

*Our choices make up our character
and who we are as individuals*

MARILYN GUIER

ISBN 978-1-64670-517-7 (Paperback)
ISBN 978-1-64670-518-4 (Digital)

Covenant Books, Inc.
11661 Hwy 707
Murrells Inlet, SC 29576
www.covenantbooks.com

To my wonderful family, Karen, Pat, Ken, Kathy, Scott, and friends who encouraged me and gave me good feedback and who show their dedication to God, country, and humanity every day by their good choices. I am blessed.

My Life so Far

I grew up in Webster Groves, Missouri, where I always felt safe. We walked with our friends to the local movie theater on Friday evenings and walked to the tennis courts on Saturdays. I remember one Friday night my parents decided to go with us to the movies. I tried to explain that Friday nights were kids' night, but to no avail. Dad was going.

The noise level from teenagers was pretty loud, and Dad stood up and yelled, "Quiet."

There were about two minutes of silence, and then the noise and laughter started again. My dad joined in the laughter. Needless to say, my parents did not attend a Friday night movie again.

My brother, sister, and I were raised in a Christian home where Sundays were spent attending church and having family time. Weekly dinners were spent around the table, with us kids talking about school and friends and my Dad telling about things he did when he was young. My mother was a great pianist, and when we were little, she would play a piece called "Rustic Dance." We knew it was time to get on our pj's when she played this piece. Then we would walk up the stairs, and in the middle of the piece she would stop playing and we would come back down the stairs. This continued several times, and when she finished the piece, it was understood that we better be in bed.

My parents never preached to us; instead, they showed their Christian belief in their kindness to others and their daily living. As kids, we always showed them the respect they deserved. Of course, we did silly things, but never anything we were ashamed of. We went to public schools, and every year our high school put on the pageant play for the school and the community. There were two full choirs and a beautiful play about the birth of Christ. It was a wonderful way to start off the Christmas season.

I attended college to get a teaching degree. I remember my dad saying, "Now don't choose a husband just because he's a good dancer." But I knew what he really meant—choose someone with good values. I fell in love, married, and have five wonderful children. When my children were young, I taught Sunday school and Vacation Bible School. And when my children were in high school, I worked as a teacher's aide with the Special School District in a grade school, a junior high school, and a high school. Each time they moved me to a different school, I asked, "Is this a promotion or a demotion?" Then I worked in a grade school for sixteen years and loved it.

After retirement, I joined the Oasis organization as a volunteer who helps children learn to read. Recently I finished seventeen years with Oasis. I am now eighty-three years old, and God has blessed me with five wonderful children, three sons-in-law, two daughters-in-law, a granddaughter-in-law, and eight grandchildren. I started writing down some stories of my life for my children to read, and before I knew it, I had written a book.

My one daughter sent me this text: "Mom your book was full of hope, inspiring, and enjoyable to read. Even if it just changes one person's life, you need to get it out there to be read. You've changed my life. I look forward to reading it again and again."

CHAPTER 1

I have been teaching a special class called Choices for fifteen years to students in their senior year of high school. I was a social studies teacher when I realized many students were not interested in learning, and so I came up with this idea of Choices. My students were not engaged in classroom discussions, spent time on social media on phones in class, hoping I would not see what they were doing, and were not completing assignments. Class is about listening and engaging with the teacher and each other, and when they are on their phones, they can't do either one and therefore they can't learn.

I went to the superintendent of the Cory School District, Dr. Sandiford, and said, "We need to do something different."

His response was, "Things are working just fine, and we do not have the money to start something new that has not been tested."

I have a strong personality, and that was not the answer I wanted.

After weeks of pestering him and explaining my plan, he finally said I could have this class for one year with no extra pay. I grabbed at the chance and started laying out my plans over the summer.

Many of my social studies students knew the answers to questions I asked but didn't feel their answers were that important and refused to raise their hands or participate in class. So when I started this new class, I decided to give an A to any student who would participate by giving an answer when called upon. I called it "An A for the Day," and class participation improved.

Fifteen years later, we have produced so many graduates and professional people, and I am so very proud of all of them. This will be my last year before I retire, and then I will pass the class on to another teacher. I will really miss working with these wonderful students. I have learned so much from them.

I'm ready for my final year of teaching these great students. It is so much fun to see them start the year not yet knowing what this class is all about and then to see them end the year with so much pride in themselves and with a renewed outlook on all the possibilities that life has to offer when they make good choices.

Today is August 15th, the first day of class. A whole new group of students will soon be in my classroom, wondering what the class will do for them. I have put a name tag on each desk and have a chart to help me identify each student. I know their thoughts will be "What are we doing with name tags on our desks? We are not in grade school." It makes it easier and faster for me to learn their names.

Everything I do has a purpose, and I hope again this year to bring out the best in these new students.

CHAPTER 2

"Good morning, class. I am Mrs. Andrews, and this class is about choices. Welcome to all of you, and please take the seat with your name on it. The name tags are for my benefit to learn your names faster, and in time you can remove them. I will enjoy getting to know each and every one of you. I really enjoy teaching this subject, and I hope that when the year is over, you will realize how your life can be great when you make good choices.

"Now I have written two phrases on the board. These phrases are 'You can choose to make bad choices and you can have your picture in the paper with the world remembering you with hate and distaste' or 'You can choose to make good choices and you can have your picture in the paper and be remembered with honor and wonder.' Now, open your notebooks and copy what is written on the board with your full name on the first line.

"In this class you can earn an A for the day by answering some of the questions that I will ask of you. This will count as 30 percent of your total grade. When I give an A to a student, I will record that A beside your name on my list. Today we are going to talk about honesty. Who wants to tell me the definition of honesty? Nate, in your mind what is the definition of honesty?"

"I think it's being truthful."

"Good answer, Nate. Give yourself an A for the day. Should someone be honest and truthful in all situations? Hannah?"

"Yes, in reality they should."

"Let's say someone asks you if you think their artwork is great, but in your mind, you don't really think it's that great. Should you be honest and hurt their feelings or lie and say yes?"

"Well, I guess I'd say yes because I don't want to hurt their feelings."

"So you're not being honest, right?"

"I guess so."

"Now the moment they ask you if their artwork is great, can you think of something honest to say to that person?"

"I guess I could say something nice about some of the things in the picture if I think that, and I suppose that would be an honest remark."

"Give yourself an A for the day. So in most situations, we can be honest without hurting someone's feelings. Suppose your teacher asks if you saw someone cheating on a test and the teacher knows you know who it is. Eric, what would you say to the teacher when asked who it is and it turns out this is a good friend?"

"Well, I don't believe in cheating, but I don't want to lose my friend. Let me think on this for a minute or two."

I could see that Eric was thinking hard for an answer.

"I guess I'd have to say I know who it is, but I have to talk to that person first and then hope the teacher would let me do that."

"So what would you say to your friend?"

"I'd say, 'You have put me in a difficult situation, and I want you to let the teacher know what you did' and hope he understands."

"Good answer and an honest one. Give yourself an A."

We continued on for the rest of the hour, and I could tell this was going to be another great year.

"Your homework for tomorrow is to write a paper about honesty and what it means to you. There's the bell, class is dismissed."

CHAPTER 3

I am ready for day two, and I hope my students are ready and prepared for another interesting day.

"Good morning, class, today we are going to check on names of students. I know many of you already know each other's names, but some of you are new so we will start off and see who knows whom. Ethan, what is the name of the student sitting in the third row fourth seat from the front?"

"I don't know him."

"So how would you learn his name?"

"I guess someone would have to tell me."

"Shane, how would Ethan learn that student's name?"

"By getting up and looking at his name tag on his desk."

"Give yourself an A for the day, Shane. Now when you students come to class each day, you are to learn everyone's name in this room. The following week, I want you to be able to tell me one thing of interest about each person."

I had some of the students read their papers that they wrote about honesty, and I was amazed at what they wrote and I let them know I was very pleased with their papers. Some had written some interesting remarks.

One student wrote, "Honesty is not a problem if you never get caught and if you're smarter than most people." Another student wrote, "I have never known an honest person." Very interesting remarks; I hope those answers will change after completing this class. I know I'll enjoy reading and grading the rest of them tonight.

CHAPTER 4

Life has funny twists and turns, and I'm on my way to meet a very important person in my life—my husband, Paul, of forty-five years who did a lot of traveling for the train company where he worked for forty years. Our five children are scattered all over the United States, so it's just the two of us learning how to enjoy life together after his retirement.

We do manage to travel to see the families in the summer, and we have a big cruise planned for my retirement next summer. Our children, their spouses, grandkids—all twenty of us will be on one ship together. I can't wait. It will be a great way to celebrate. My son-in-law Mark loves to travel and has made all the arrangements for all of us. So happy I don't have to make the plans and can just enjoy the trip.

CHAPTER 5

"Class, I have a story to tell you today, so just relax and listen. Before I became a social studies teacher, I worked for the Special Education District in our town. They had just started a new program putting special-ed students into a senior high school. We had a room that used to be the loading ramp for the school until they enclosed it with glass windows. We froze in the wintertime and had to keep our coats around us during class.

"We had six students who were mentally and physically challenged. These students had very little going for them, but they were happy and willing to try hard to improve. One student was in a wheel-chair and had a large tumor on his back that fit into a special area of the wheelchair. Every morning when I would help him off the school bus, he would say to me, 'This is going to be a great day.' How could any able-bodied person have a bad day if he could always look forward to a great day?

"We had asked different teachers if they would accept some of our students into their classrooms. Only a gym teacher and a chemistry teacher offered to take a student. The gym teacher offered to take one boy. Each day I would take him down to the gym, and the teacher would line the students up and call out their names for attendance. One by one he called every name, except for my student's name.

"I would then take my student out into the hall with a basketball, and I would dribble the ball around his wheelchair and tell him to try and get the ball. He would laugh and try his hardest to get that ball. After class, the teacher would come out of the gym and turn the other way from us. We began saying "Hi" each time he came out of class, and he would never acknowledge us. I told my student that we were going to continue to say "Hi" and see how long it would take him to answer us. Well, it took seven months.

"During the winter when the weather was too bad to go outside, the students gathered in the gym. I would show up with one student in a wheelchair carrying a basketball in his lap. A group of boys wanted to use the basketball, and I told them, 'Okay, as long as my student got to play.' I have to say the boys were very good to him.

"The chemistry teacher said she would take two of our students because her one class was not the smartest class and our students would be comfortable there. At the end of the school year, these two students were each given a D+.

"To them it didn't matter that it was a D+. It was a grade on a report card which was something they had never had before. It was like Christmas excitement for them. Their hard work had paid off. These kids have very little going for them, except for small things they work hard to get, but those small things make them excited and happy.

"You all are very privileged with good physical and mental health. Are you willing to work as hard as these students? I hope you are because you can accomplish so much in life if you do."

CHAPTER 6

For my lesson today, I contacted the principal at Richmond High School in the next town to volunteer one of their senior students. He was more than willing to help with my plan and asked me to be sure to let him know how it turned out. Today my students will be learning about appearances.

I arrived to school early and made out a name tag for our new student, and I added a desk for her in the fourth row in front of Susan, now it was time for class.

"We have a new student today from a different school district. I want you all to welcome her to class. This is Sara Wilson. Sara, please take a seat in the fourth row where you will see your name tag."

Sara and I did a great job to make Sara look different from all the other students in this class. She has a black hairdo with curls all over her head, makeup, an outfit I sewed together with a zipper up the back and a little padding underneath, a gathered print skirt, a wide belt, white blouse, and saddle shoes with white socks. She looks perfect, just how I wanted her to look, and you should see the faces on my students; they must think she's from Mars. Just the response I wanted from my class.

"Would anyone like to ask Sara a question?"

No response.

"Sara, would you like to introduce yourself to the class?"

"Yes, I'm Sara Wilson, and we just moved here from the Richmond School District two days ago. I was a senior there, and I like to sing and dance."

"Sara, do you want to say anything else?"

"No thank you."

"Well, Sara, we have a harvest dance coming up next week, and it doesn't give you much time to really get to know anyone, so would one of you nice gentleman or ladies like to escort Sara to the dance?"

No hands up.

"Mark, what about you?"

"I already asked Joan, Mrs. Andrews."

"Sam, how about you?"

"Well, I wasn't planning on going because I have other plans that night."

"Well, Sara, we'll just have to work on finding you a date."

Annie's hand flew up and she said, "Mrs. Andrews, I am going with some friends that don't have dates and Sara can come with us if she wants to."

"Sara, is that all right with you?"

"Yes, that would be nice."

"Annie, talk to Sara after class and put an A in your notebook."

I gave the class a few minutes to talk with each other, and I noticed Annie was the only one talking with Sara.

"Okay, class, it's time to get to work."

The rest of the day went well, and I was excited to see what tomorrow would bring.

CHAPTER 7

"I see our new student is absent today, and I would like to have a discussion about your thoughts on Sara Wilson. Annie, you were talking to Sara during class and after class yesterday. What kind of an impression did you get?"

"I like her. She was bright, and after school, she gave me a little bit of her song-and-dance routine."

"So were you offended by her appearance and dress?"

"Well, no, not really because I dressed a little strange in seventh grade. She was sweet."

"So appearances didn't matter?"

"No."

Just then, another new student came into the classroom; she had blonde hair, very pretty, and dressed like all my students.

"Class, I would like to introduce our new student to you."

I could see the boy's eyes popping out.

"This is Sara Wilson, same name as the first new student we had yesterday. She's a straight-A student from Richmond School, she was prom queen two years in a row, has been offered a full scholarship to an Ivy League school, MIT, majoring in physics. She also has performed at the Muny Opera House in Forrest Park, and she will most likely be valedictorian of her class at graduation this year."

You could see the rest of my students' mouths fly open.

"Sara was very nice to help me put on this lesson on appearances. Let this be a good lesson in life—get to know a person before you form an opinion. Thanks to Annie, she had the right idea to get to know Sara before forming her opinion. Annie, give yourself two A's for the day."

CHAPTER 8

"Today I am wearing a different shoe on each of my feet. Take a good look at my right foot and tell me what you see? Jacob, what do you see?"

"A foot."

"Describe the foot."

"Well, it has a white sock and a shoe that has brown and white leather."

"Hailey, what else do you see?"

"I'm not sure I see anything else."

"Kaitlyn?"

"I see ribs in the white sock."

"Now look at my left foot. What do you see different about this one? Eric?"

"I see a white sock, no ribs, and it's turned down."

"Anything else? Tryon."

"I see a dark leather shoe."

"Good, now does anyone see differences in the two? Brenda."

"Yes, the first shoe does not have its sock turned down and the shoes are different."

"Good, now I want to share a story from my school days with you. I attended Cornell High School, and all the girls wore their socks straight up, not rolled down, and we all wore saddle shoes, as they were called. And if you could afford them the brand name was Spalding saddle shoes. I wore a fake brand, and that was sort of acceptable.

"We had a new girl in our school that moved from Chicago, and she wore white socks turned down with dark shoes. So what, you say. Well, if you did not dress like the 'in crowd,' you were shunned. Our school had sororities, and they could make a person feel unwanted if you did not dress the same. She was not making friends and did not understand why.

"My friends and I felt sorry for her and decided to talk to her about our accepted dress code of shoes and socks. We enjoyed her and soon invited her to join our sorority. Brenda, why do you think I shared this story with the class?"

"You wanted us to see the person from the inside and not the outside."

"Give yourself an A. Always remember to get to know someone first before you form an opinion. You never know, that person might become your best friend. I'm very proud of all of you and your wonderful working minds. I hope you'll carry this lesson with you the rest of your lives."

CHAPTER 9

"Today is the day we learn how many students in this class you know by their first name. Ethan, have you learned all your classroom buddies' names?"

"Yes."

"Name them for me starting with the first row."

Ethan named each student.

"Great job, Ethan, and how did you learn them?"

"By asking them in the hallways, I did know some of them before we started this class, and I learned the others by looking at their name tags."

"So, Shane's answer the other day helped."

"Yes, I guess I sounded a little stupid then."

"I do not think anyone in this class is stupid, we are just learning new ways to do things and solve problems. Good job, Ethan, give yourself an A. Okay, now we'll start with Susan in the first row and go through each student."

Each one had learned every student's first name, and I'm very proud of all of them.

At the end of class, I reminded them that they had to learn something interesting about each class-mate by next Friday. I hoped they all would be able to do it. I'm falling in love with each student again this year. I hope each parent knows how special their child is.

CHAPTER 10

It's Friday and time for show-and-tell. I always look forward to this day because I have the privilege of learning more about my students. It's amazing what great things they find out about their classmates. As the students take their seats, I can tell they are ready to talk about the interesting things they have learned about each other; most everyone has a smile on their face.

"Today I'm not going to call on anyone to start. I am going to choose Kaitlyn to come up in front and choose who she would like to be first, second, and so on. When your name is called, you are to tell about one classmate who has not already been chosen. Let's hope the last student is well prepared. Okay, let the sharing begin."

Kaitlyn chose Sam to go first. He picked Sara and told how she had enjoyed going skiing last winter in Colorado for the first time and ended up on the experienced slope, thinking she was on the beginners' slope. She started down the slope and lost a ski and did a summersault the rest of the way down. She has been able to laugh about it when she tells the story.

Next, Kaitlyn chose Zac. Zac picked Ethan and told about a time when Ethan had been in grade school and the teacher had all the boys and girls run a race together. A classmate named Kathy came in ahead of him and got first place. He said he was not happy about that, so he told the teacher it wasn't fair and he wanted to run against her again. So the teacher had the two of them run again, and she won. He said he learned to not run against her anymore.

"Did you learn anything else, Ethan?"

"Yes, I learned I should have congratulated her and walked away."

"Good answer, Ethan."

Next, Kaitlyn chose Nina. Nina picked Kathy, and she told about a time when she was in grade school and they were to dress like one of the pilgrims or an Indian for their Thanksgiving program. Kathy chose to dress like an Indian, and when she got to class, she found out she had the wrong day. The teacher was so nice and had her model the outfit so the other students would know how to dress, but Kathy said she was embarrassed at the time.

Next, Kaitlyn chose Sam and he chose Nate. Sam told about when Nate was on vacation with his family in Colorado boating down a river in a canoe. They were going through some pretty fast rapids and were surprised they made it safely through. They stopped on a sandbar to rest and saw another canoe that turned over coming down the same rapids. They waded out in the water; grabbed the canoe, ice chest, and other belongings; and waited for the boys to come to the sandbar.

Nate and his father built a fire to help dry the boys out, and then they all shared their food. He said he remembered it was a fun part of their vacation.

I could see the class was enjoying this assignment, and I was also. We just finished before the bell rang, and I had to give an A to everyone for such a good and enjoyable hour.

CHAPTER 11

I was sitting in the teacher's lounge finishing my lesson plans for the next day when Mary, the new English teacher, sat down beside me. She did not look at all happy. She said she was having a hard time dealing with some unruly students in her class and wasn't sure how to handle it. She asked me if I had any suggestions.

"Well, Mary, are you making your lessons interesting or just going by the book?"

"What do you mean?"

"Are you doing some fun things that your students can relate to and still be learning? Make a game of English. Try having them write some funny sentences and giving the paper to another student to punctuate. Try that tomorrow and see if it helps the unruly ones behave better, but be prepared for laughter."

"Interesting idea. I'll give it a try tomorrow."

CHAPTER 12

"Today I want to thank all of you for the time you spent getting to know each other with your wonderful stories last Friday. I have learned so much about each one of you, and I will treasure each and every one in my memory. I hope you all have taken away some good memories too.

"Today let's talk about memories and what helps each one of us remember things. Memory is keeping a mental record of different experiences you've had in your life. It can be a process of learning different skills like sports, driving a car, using a sewing machine, using tools, or cooking. It can be remembering a verbal response like what your mother told you to do after school today or answers to a test you're going to take. Or it can be an emotional response like missing someone you grew up with when they moved away or a fight you had with a good friend.

"Our brains work in different ways to remember things, and some of us have unique ways of helping our memories work. So today I would like to know how you remember things. What method works for you? Do I see any hands? Who would like to go first? Hannah?"

"I keep repeating things I want to remember. I'll do it about a dozen times."

"Jacob?"

"I try to associate something with the things I want to remember, like the name of a new person I've just met, so I'll think of someone else I know by that name or something that reminds me of that name."

"Deion?"

"I write it down on paper, and then I can visualize it later."

"Anyone else? No. Now, how many of you use the repeating method to remember? Raise your hands. Seven. Now, how many associate something else with what you want to remember? Ten. How many of you write it down? I count seven. What about you, Shane, how do you remember things?"

"I guess I just have a good memory because I don't use any method."

"Well, Shane, you are very lucky and blessed to have such a great memory. I, like the other seven, have to write it down, and then I can also visualize it on that paper. Great job, class."

Chapter 13

"Good morning, class, it's good to see so many smiling faces. Today I would like each one of you to take out your cell phones and hold them in the air. Thank you. You may put your cell phones down on the desk.

"I would like you to check every entry you may have on your phone for the whole day yesterday from morning until midnight. And note the time spent on each number. Let's say you sent a text to someone and it took ten seconds and you received a text back and it took you three seconds to read it, so you would mark down thirteen seconds in your notes. Or you talked on your phone for ten minutes, mark down ten minutes. Mark down how much time you spent on social media, texting, and the internet. Write down the amount of time, and please be honest about all the time you spent on the phone. When you're finished, write it on a piece of paper with your name."

I noticed everyone working hard, and some are smiling at what they're reading on their phones.

"I don't want you to hurry with this assignment. It's very important that you be honest."

Some have finished rather quickly, and others are taking more time. I told those that had finished to read or to finish homework from another class.

"Now that everyone seems to be finished, we will start with Sam and go down each row, telling how many hours and minutes you came up with."

I guess I shouldn't be surprised at the hours spent on their phones, but it seems to increase each year.

"Mark, you win the prize for most time on the phone, you are a slave to that phone. Okay, class, thank you for your honesty. Now tomorrow you are not to use your phones at all.

"My, what sad faces I see. I will make an exception for you taking calls from your parents or if you have to report to them, but no other calls, texting, social media, etc. I would also like each one of you to let your parents know you are not to use your phone for anything else.

"This assignment is very important, and I know it will be hard for you to do, but please no use of phones. I was going to collect your phones, but I trust each and every one of you to do the right thing. This assignment ends at midnight tomorrow night."

CHAPTER 14

"This whole class did such a great job with your phones, so I have put a treat on everyone's desk, feel free to enjoy it. Now, cell phones, if used properly, can be a great tool as long as you don't overdo it. Never use your cell phone to avoid conversations in person with friends and family and never let it interfere with doing wonderful things. You also need to avoid putting places where you're going, your name, friends' names, and what your schedule is during each day on your phone.

"Now I have two articles to read to you. The first one is about a girl that was killed in St. Charles."

> *Body of missing St. Charles student found in a wooded area. Jamey Larson was found murdered yesterday. Her mother told the press, "Jamey had a boy friend named*

Joey although I had never met him." Her daughter told her Joey had invited her to see a movie after school on Friday. Jamey's mother gave her daughter permission because she thought Joey was a classmate of Jamey's.

When the police questioned her friends there was no boyfriend named Joey in their group of friends.

"Now for the second article."

Murder suspect found in St. Charles. George Smith was apprehended yesterday and charged with the murder of Jamey Larson. Jamey had been on her phone and computer with this man thinking he was a 16-year-old boy named Joey. Smith, a 45-year-old employed banker, had been preying on young girls for a long time using information he was able to get from social media, cell phones, and passwords on their computers. At this time we have no idea how many girls he may have murdered.

"Now I'll repeat what I said earlier. How many of you put everything you do during the day on social media, pictures of you and your friends, in a way that reveal your house and school? How many post information about what your schedule is for the day? This is the way predators get your information. A cell phone and a computer are great tools if used with caution.

"When my husband was ill and in a rehab facility, I got a phone call from some man whose voice I thought I recognized as one of my husband's friends from out of town. I called him by name. 'Hi, John,' and he said, 'I just talked to Paul. I told him my daughter is having some money problems and I don't get my social security check until the end of the month and could he lend me six hundred dollars? I will pay him back when I receive my check. Paul said to call you.' I said, 'How do I send the money?' He told me to go to Walmart and get a money order, and he gave me an address in Michigan. Well, thank goodness my brain kicked in and I tried to call my husband, but there was no answer. So I drove over to the rehab and told my husband about the call.

"Paul said that he had a call too, but the man asked him for a six-thousand-dollar loan. The caller was nobody Paul knew, so he hung up. I went home and tried to look up our local police department but could not find their phone number. I did find the FBI number, so I called and explained my problem. They told me to call my local police department and gave me the phone number.

"I called, told them my problem, and they asked if I wanted a policeman to come to the house, and I said, 'Yes, I guess.' A nice young policeman came to the house, and as I was telling him the story the phone rang. It was the man who had called asking for money. I gave the phone to the officer. The officer listened and then said, 'This is the police, and don't you call this young woman again.' The man let out a lot of curse words and hung up. He said many of these calls come from other countries, making them hard to trace. The officer took the address the caller had given me and left.

"About an hour later, there was a knock at my door, and I was afraid to answer it. I looked out the window and saw that it was the same officer that I had talked with in my home. He said, 'I thought you would like to know that I called the police in the town in Michigan from the address you gave me. They said they have the house under surveillance.'

"I thanked him for taking the time to let me know. I was so glad I used my brain and not my emotions that were telling me to help a friend of my husband's. But there is something I have never been able to figure out and that is how he got my husband's phone number at the rehab facility and my home phone number. How did he make the connection between a landline at a different location and a cell phone?

"Now, what have you learned from this story? Hailey?"

"Be safe and not sorry. Use your brain and not your emotions."

"Good answer, A for the day. Please don't let your emotions make you become another Jamey Larson. Predators prey on our emotions to get what they want. We need our brains to help us make good choices and decisions. I used my emotion to say the name of a friend on the phone, and then after the caller told me what he wanted, my brain started working and I was able to make good decisions. This is what predators do with information from your computer and phones. They're at it, twenty-four hours a day, seven days a week.

"A teacher I worked with received a call about her grandson, telling her he was in an accident out of town and she needed to wire ten thousand dollars for his care in the hospital. She was so worried and upset, she let her emotions make the decision and not her brain. When she finally made a decision to call her son to ask about her grandson, she found out the expensive mistake she had made."

CHAPTER 15

"Today we have a very interesting gentleman here to talk to all of you, and maybe some of you have heard about him. He's Dave Hammerstein, captain of the Oakfield Basketball Team. They perform all over the world and will be playing a game today in the gym for the whole school. Each senior classroom has a player from the team talking to them today. Please give a hand to Mr. Hammerstein."

"Thank you, Mrs. Andrews," Dave stated. "Mrs. Andrews asked me five years ago if our team would be willing to talk to senior students. It was the first time I had been asked to do something like this, and I was nervous. I almost declined, and then I remembered her words, 'You may be saving another life by your words.' I told myself get over my nerves and do it.

"I was a big football player in high school and had a football scholarship to the University of

Missouri in the fall. I cannot tell you how excited I was, and I could hardly wait for the summer to end. My friends and I loved to dare each other to do things, and that was pretty much what we did to pass the time when we weren't working at the fast food restaurant or the auto shop in town.

"One day we were talking about driving through a red light just after it changed from yellow and making it through without being hit. We talked about timing it just right because the cars going the other way would have a few seconds' delay. I decided one day to give it a try and asked my buddy to film it to show to the other guys.

"As soon as I saw the light turn red, I hit the gas to speed through it. I thought no one was coming from the other way, but at the last second, a large truck came down that lane and hit the driver's side of my car.

"The front dashboard tore into my legs, and the door cut through some of the bone in my back. I heard myself scream, and then the EMTs were cutting me out of the car. I was rushed to the hospital where they decided they could not save my legs and removed them at the knees. The next day, I realized I was paralyzed from the waist down. I prayed to God that this was a dream and I would wake up soon. But

I realized it was real and I knew my life was over. I wondered why God didn't take my life at the time of the accident. No football, my life's dream, no walking again, I felt that there was nothing to live for. I fell into a deep depression.

"After two months in the hospital, I was sent to rehab where I refused to do any of the exercises they had planned for me. Why should I do them when I felt I was just a vegetable? One day, a therapist came into my room and said, 'You're wasting a good life. Get out of that bed and into your wheelchair and come with me.' I thought, 'Who does this guy think he is?'

"We headed down to the therapy room, and he took off his jacket and pulled off his slacks. He had on shorts and a T-shirt, and where his right arm and left leg were supposed to be were prosthetics. He said, 'I lost these fighting in Afghanistan, fighting a war. How did you lose yours?'

"'By making a very bad choice,' I said.

"'Okay, now it's time to make some good choices. It took me a long time to decide to change my attitude and decide I could do so much with my life if I had the determination and guts to do so. We both have lost limbs on our bodies but haven't lost our minds and our ability to live a life of production. Now what was your goal in life before your accident?'

"'I was going to be the best football player ever and I had a scholarship to University of Missouri.'

"'So what was your second choice to do besides football?'

"'I didn't have a second choice.'

"'Well, now you have one, and it's to realize you have been given a second chance at life so make the most of it.'

"I thought this guy sounded like and acted like a sergeant in the Marines, and I was not interested. I was not going to listen to him. He said, 'We are starting with these exercises now. I do not listen to any excuses so get to work.' He was a hard trainer with lots of guts and was not willing to listen to any sob stories. I learned to work hard, and my depression was less and less each day. I had worked so hard, I was gaining some feeling in my waist. I was fitted with new prosthetics legs but told I would always have to use a walker or a wheelchair. One day, Dave asked me if I had ever played basketball and I said, 'A little bit.'

"'How would you like to try out for the Oakfield Basketball team?' he asked. I said that I had never heard of them. He told me that they are a team of paraplegic players that play all over the world. They have these great specially made wheelchairs that you learn to use as you would your own body and said that if I was interested, he could get me in touch with the coach for an interview and a tryout.

"I started working hard at making baskets and improving my body, and two years later I was on the team. It's been the love of my life and so rewarding to meet people who have not given up on life but have worked hard and made good choices. I made a bad choice in high school, but I learned to make good choices that have made me a better person. Make sure your choices are good ones.

"Thanks for letting me tell my story and I hope it makes all of you think before you make bad choices in life. Now I think it's time for your class to head to the gym so we basketball players can show you how the game is played. And today the game is free."

Chapter 16

Charley, a student of mine, always sat in the back of the classroom and had been very quiet since the first day of school. On the first day of class, I was standing by the door to welcome each student when he poked his head in the door and said, "I don't want to be here, and you can't make me," and then walked away.

I looked out the door to see where he was going, and he stood there, saying, "Fooled ya, didn't I?" He was repeating his senior year because he was hospitalized last year after his girlfriend broke up with him, and he fell into a deep depression.

This morning, Charley asked if he could talk to me after school, and I told him I would be happy to talk with him and I would be in my classroom waiting. I did feel sorry for him, and I was glad he felt comfortable enough to come and talk with me.

When he met me after school, he said, "I'm not sure what to say, but I have to talk to someone. My parents are divorced, and I really hate my dad."

I asked him why he had such a hatred for his father.

"My dad should never have divorced my mother. She cries all the time, and I feel so sorry for her."

I asked him if his parents got along and if it was a happy home. He said no and that they fought all the time.

"So you would feel better and like your dad if they stayed together and were unhappy and fought all the time?"

"Well, no, but I don't like it this way either."

"Your father probably thought it was better for you and your mom if he left. Some people just don't get along in a marriage. Sometimes it is because of their different personalities or a lot of baggage they had before they were married. It has nothing to do with you. What do you feel you've lost since your dad moved out?"

"I have a feeling of not belonging. I feel lost, my life is dark, and I am filled with hate and anger."

"Tell me some things you haven't lost."

"I can't."

"Well, let's start with the love of your mother and the love of your father, although you're not feeling that right now. You will eventually learn it is true. You have friends, school, food, and a place of shelter. These are all good things to have.

"Sometimes it is very hard for some personalities to get along, and it's better to be divorced. It's a very hard adjustment for you and for your mom. She feels rejected and probably doesn't know what she is going to do with the rest of her life, but when the tears stop, she will realize it was all for the best, and so will you.

"Divorce doesn't mean your dad loves you any less, and he still needs your support very much. You need to let both of them know how much you care for them, and when your mother starts to complain to you about your dad or your father complains to you about your mother, you need to tell them not to talk to you about each other because you love both of your parents."

"I guess you're right. I'll try and do what you said, but it won't be easy."

"No, it won't be easy, but you have to try. That's all I'm asking you to do."

"Thanks, Mrs. Andrews, for taking the time to talk to me. I've really been hurting."

"Thank you, Charley, for trusting me enough to tell me what's been bothering you. I knew there was something going on in your life because you were so quiet in my class. I hope I have helped you, and you know that you can talk to me anytime. What you say will never be discussed with anyone else."

CHAPTER 17

"Today we will be making plans to visit three different facilities in our town that can use some help. I will divide you all into three groups to help at the Seacrest Shelter, KG Pantry, and the South Wood Village Nursing Home. You are to spend one week at each facility and get involved in the care and help that each facility provides. When everyone has had a chance to visit all three facilities, I will expect a paper on what you have learned from this experience, so you might want to make notes as you go along. If you go with the right attitude, you will be well rewarded with a new outlook on life."

They all seemed relaxed about this experience and I hoped things would go well. This is a good group of kids. I need to let each parent know how great their child is and what a great job they did raising them. I'm so proud of them; I feel like they are my very own.

We spent the rest of the day forming the three groups and explaining what some of their jobs would be at each facility. I told them they were to get to know the volunteers, the workers, and the people they would be helping. The people from these agencies have always been wonderful to my students and have seemed very happy to have them help out.

"When you signed up for this class, you agreed to trade your study hall time to participate in this exercise. You will be gone to these facilities right before this class and returning after your study hall class. Please bring a lunch to eat at the agency where you are to meet for the day. Please bring your permission slips signed by a parent tomorrow."

CHAPTER 18

All my students remembered their permission slips, and each group was ready to go to their assigned agency. They left ten minutes ago on the school buses. I will be checking on as many as I can today. These are life lessons they will carry with them the rest of their lives. So many kids live in their own cocoons and never realize how fortunate they are with their health and home life. Today and this week, they will learn the value of their own lives and may even come up with ideas for their lives in the future.

I have one grandson who spent the summer of his junior year of college on a pineapple plantation in Hawaii picking pineapples, sleeping on a cot at night in the open air with just a canvas overhead, and walking miles to a store or another plantation to visit with other kids. He graduated this spring and is now in Vietnam, teaching English. He never realized this would be something he would be doing when he was younger. He thought he would be a baseball player. Life has so much to offer.

Chapter 19

Three weeks have gone by so fast, and I have really missed my students. I hope they have learned lessons from these agencies, their clients, and the many volunteers who give their time each day helping people.

"It's great to have you all back in class today, and I hope you are ready to tell us about your assignments on the agencies you visited. I hope this was a good experience for all of you. Who would like to go first and tell about your experience volunteering at the Seacrest Shelter? Nate?"

"I was very surprised that some of the people had good jobs that they lost during the economy downturn. Then they lost their savings because of bad loans and investments. Now they have large debts to pay off, their cars and homes were repossessed, and they are living in the shelter. I have to say I thought people in shelters were just bums that didn't want to work. I didn't think something like this could really happen to people."

"Melinda?"

"I talked with one lady whose husband had left her and her two children, cleaned out their bank accounts, and left her with debts to pay. She lost her house, and she and her children ended up in the Seacrest Shelter. I was also surprised that something like this could happen."

"Deion?"

"I met a young man just a little older than me who lost his parents and his home. Coming home from his job, a gang attacked him on the street and broke his leg, a rib, and he lost part of his hearing. After his hospital stay, he came back to the shelter where he had been staying until he could make enough money to stay in an apartment. Man, what a sad situation for him. I told him I would check on him now and then to see how he was doing."

"Thank you, Deion, what a nice thing to do. So we have learned that people can be down on their luck by outside circumstances, and that doesn't mean they are lazy people. Now who would like to tell about the KG Pantry? Shane?"

"I was surprised at how much food people donate to the pantry each and every day and how hard the volunteers work to give their clients food for a week or two. They seem to know them by name and greet them like friends. We really didn't get a chance to do some serious talking to the clients, but some of the workers said, they were people just down on their luck. They had low-paying jobs and had a hard time paying for their rent and food. Some were very embarrassed to ask for help.

"The people that we gave the food to were so very thankful and seemed to appreciate the food they received. I thought they just gave out food, but one of the workers said, because of generous donations, they can help with rent, college scholarships, and they have a birthday club where they give birthday gifts to the clients' children. It really surprised me that they do so much to help people."

"Nina?"

"My feelings are the same as Shane's, but I did meet a woman whose husband left her with no funds to care for herself and her five children. She was working two low-paying jobs to get by and did not know what she would do if she didn't have the help of the KG Pantry."

"So again, we are finding out that these people could be our own families if misfortune hits us. Our society needs to show them help and love. Next we have the South Wood Village Nursing Home. Sam?"

"I met a war veteran from the Vietnam War, and he was so very interesting. He told me that he really didn't like to talk about the war, but he felt that a young person like me should know what war was like so maybe I could help keep our country from going to war in the future. I have to say, some of the stories were pretty scary, and he didn't hold back on some of the bad stuff, but he sure made an impression on me. He told me my generation needs to work to bring peace to our world."

"Jamey?"

"I met a chemistry teacher, and she said she loved working with her students but felt that students today didn't show respect for education like they did back when she was teaching. She told a story about one of her students that tried mixing the wrong chemicals and almost blew up her classroom. She said she was happy no one got hurt and her student was in tears for the mess she had caused. She had many great stories to tell, and I loved hearing them. She was fun and so interesting."

"See how much you can learn from older people? Talk to your grandparents, older people, and see what interesting lives they have had. I'm sure they will educate you with wonderful stories of their experiences in life.

"Class, I have enjoyed every one of your comments about your visits to these important agencies. There are such great things to learn from people of all walks of life. Thanks to you wonderful students, you have made my day, and I will enjoy reading your papers tonight.

"Since you all have been working so hard on this assignment, I would like to treat you all to a pizza party during class on Friday. I think it's time we had a game day and pizza. Students, please get together and plan a game, and I'll provide the pizza. Hand in a piece of paper with the kind of pizza you like, and I will try my best to get those kinds. Enjoy the rest of the day."

Chapter 20

Friday came, and the pizza was delivered by the time the students were in class. They had chosen the game Hangman, which surprised me because it's such an old game. They had fun making up funny five-word sentences, and the laughter and joking didn't stop until the hour was over. It was a fun day for me just to see them having such a good time. We all need these fun times in our lives.

CHAPTER 21

As I sit here grading papers, I wonder what my husband has cooked up for our meal tonight. I guess I must be getting hungry. Paul retired six years ago and has been fixing all the meals since, except for the holidays; I still do those and enjoy doing them. I told him he should have been a chef because he makes such good meat loaf, stir-fry, pork roast, beef roast, and vegetables that your taste buds think they have died and gone to heaven.

I put a note on the refrigerator that reads, "When cooking for four, make sure there are four to eat it." The meals are so good and plentiful, he eats one and I eat the other three. My mouth is already watering, so I better pack up and head for home.

CHAPTER 22

I told two of my social study students, Melinda and Joey, both juniors, to come to my classroom during their study hall to complete a test that I had given when they were out sick.

"I want you both to take a seat and get started on your test," I told them.

They were just about finished when there was a knock on the door.

Charley's head poked around the door, and he said, "Mrs. Andrews, I need to talk to you."

"I'm working with two students."

He said, "I really need to talk to you!"

"Come on in and have a seat. I hope you don't mind talking while my students are here."

My two students had just finished their exam.

Charley said, "I'm having those same feelings I had last year because another girlfriend broke up with me on Saturday."

Charley has a rough exterior but a very caring heart that breaks so easily.

Just then, Melinda spoke up and said, "I had that happen to me last year, and I cried my eyes out and my friends were so nice and helped me get over it by just talking it through."

I asked Joey if he had ever had that happen to him. He said, "Well, it was the other way around. I had to tell a girl I didn't think we should date anymore. I really felt bad about it, but when I told her, she said she was thinking the same thing, and that made me feel worse. I didn't know if she was saying that to hide her hurt or really wanted to break up also."

I told them that dating is a ritual of getting to know someone better. Sometimes you ask someone out because you think they're cute, smart, fun, etc. But after you have dated them for a while, you realize you have nothing in common. Breakups are always hard, but dating is a way of finding out what you want in a mate years later when you want to settle down with someone. It's a way of finding out if you both like the same things, enjoy each other's company for long periods of time, and if you can put up with their quirks and odd behaviors and still care for them.

The kids started sharing funny stories about dating, and I could see Charley starting to relax and enjoy the conversations, and then he started to add some funny stories himself. Before we knew it, we had talked for more than an hour. I was glad today I had a break until lunch, and I told the kids I would let their teacher know they were with me and that's why they were late to their class, but their stories were safe with me. I would not share.

Chapter 23

"Class, I'm sure you noticed I have not been calling out any A's for the day anymore during class. I will no longer be doing that, but I will be writing A's in my grade book all the time for your answers to my questions. Since this is 30 percent of your grade, you may check on those A's at the end of the week after school if you want to. You will each be given a total of the amount of A's you have at the end of each semester. Any writing assignments I give you during the year will count for 35 percent of your grade. I will be giving you one last written assignment at the end of the year, which will also count 35 percent of your grade.

"I want to be fair when giving these written assignments. I know when most of the other teachers give their student tests, and I will not be giving your assignments at the same time so I will expect your very best work. I started this class fifteen years ago. And ten years ago, I started this type of grading.

Seven of those ten years, my students have received all A's and a few A pluses. They worked hard and deserved every A. I know this class can do the same. So let's work on keeping those year-end A's going.

"I have put three words on the board this morning, and I hope you have been looking at them while I gave my little speech. Chi, will you please read them out loud?"

"Trust, honesty, truthfulness."

"Thank you."

"Now we will go through each one separately, starting with trust. What words describe *trust*? Raise your hand, and I will point to you but give me time to write them on the board."

"Exact."

"Honest."

"Sincere."

"Loyal."

"Fact."

"Speak truth."

"Proven."

"Good job, students. Now do the same for *honesty*."

"Fair."

"Truthful."

"Upright."

"Frank."

"Honest."

"Open."

"Genuine."

"Virtuous."

"Credible."

"Sincere."

"Incorruptible."

"Candid."

"Honorable."

"Now, *truthfulness*."

"Honesty."

"Justice."

"Obligation."

"Responsibility."

"Relied on."

"Will do what he says."

"Truthfulness."

"Believing."

"Faithfulness."

"What one word is in all three groups? Zac."

"Honesty."

"Raise your hand if you disagree with Zac's answer?"

No hands raised.

"So everyone agrees with Zac. So the most important word in our language is honesty. Honesty gains you respect from your family, your friends, and other people. I want you to repeat this last sentence: 'The most important word in our language is honesty,' and write it in your notebook. When I give you a written assignment, if you write this sentence at the bottom of your paper, you will receive five extra points. Thanks for your great responses today, and you are dismissed. I will see you all tomorrow."

CHAPTER 24

"I have three more words on the blackboard today, and, Shane, would you read them to the class?"

"Deceive, cheat, lie."

"I want you to do the same as you did yesterday, and we will list words underneath them. We'll start with *deceive*."

"False."

"Mislead."

"Cheat."

"Lie."

"Fool."

"Trick."

"Dupe."

"Next word is *cheat*."

"Swindle."

"Defraud."

"Trick."

"Deceive."

"Fraudulent."

"Liar."

"Imposter."

"Next word is *lie*."

"False."

"Fib."

"Untruthful."

"Deceiving."

"Liar."

"Falsehood."

"Melinda, which word stands out in each list of words?"

"Lie."

"Let's take a vote and see if anyone disagrees with Melinda. Raise your hands if you disagree. No hands again, great job. Your character is known by your honesty and good choices or by your lies and bad choices. Which will you be known for? Write that sentence in your notebook, and if you write it on your assignment paper, you will get five extra points."

CHAPTER 25

"With all the horrible shootings that have been happening around the country, I have another story to share with you. I have changed the names but not the story. When I was with the Special School District, I had a student named Bill who was in ninth grade but older than the rest of the class because he had been held back a year in school. He had not been doing any of his assignments.

"I said to him one morning, 'I want you to finish this paper before you leave class today because you haven't been completing anything.' He replied, 'I could get you.' That remark really bothered me. Some people would say that the hair stood up on the back of their neck.

"Later I told one of the other teachers about what was said, and she told me to tell the principal. I was in a hurry after school and didn't let the principal know what was said. The next morning, when I was walking down the hall to my classroom, the principal stopped me and said that the assistant principal wanted to see me in his office at 10:00 a.m.

"This was my first year teaching at that school, and I was a little worried about why he wanted to see me. At 10:00 a.m., I walked into his office, and there was my student Bill with his mother. The assistant principal asked me to tell him what was said yesterday, and I told him.

"Bill and his mother started to say something, and the assistant principal cut them off and said, 'You need to get your son help, and until you do, he is not allowed in school.' When Bill did come back to school, he was placed with another teacher. Two months after Bill came back to school, a seventh grader walked into the ninth grade study hall and shot one boy, killing him and critically wounding Bill.

"These two boys had been terrorizing the seventh grader's brother who was in their grade. That morning, he came to school with a gun in his gym bag, took an exam, making a perfect score, shot the boys, and later turned the gun on himself. I want you to ask questions about this story. I will write your questions on the board as you ask them, and then we will discuss them. Raise your hands, and I will point to you. Give me time to write them."

"Why didn't you tell the principal?"

"Who told the principal?"

"Did the ninth grader's friends know he was being terrorized, and if they did, why didn't they tell someone?"

"Did his parents know the brother was being bullied and terrorized?"

"Did the school know about the bullying?"

"Why wasn't the gun locked up so he couldn't use it?"

"Did his mother really get Bill help, or did she just tell the principal she did?"

"Why didn't the shooter tell his parents or someone older?"

"These are great questions, and they are the same questions asked in every shooting. Let's start with the first question, why I didn't tell the principal. I have often asked myself *why*. Maybe it was because I was taught not to be a tattletale or maybe I didn't want to get him in trouble and thought I could handle it myself. I really don't know the reason."

"Next question. Who told the principal? I believe it was the teacher I had talked to about Bill. She did the right thing by informing the principal. As we go through the next questions, I would like you to tell what you think the answer might be. Did the ninth grader's friends know he was being terrorized, and why didn't they tell someone? Brianna."

"The other students had to know. That kind of news travels very fast in school. But maybe they didn't tell because they just thought it would stop or they didn't want the boys picking on them if they told."

"Did his parents know the brother was being bullied and terrorized? Charley?"

"I don't think they knew he would take a gun to school and shoot someone. But they must have known something was wrong because he was probably acting different. Maybe he didn't want to tell them."

"Jerome?"

"We guys always feel we can handle things ourselves, and we don't like to show we can't—at least, that's the way I feel."

"I hope this story changes that thinking for all of you. Next question, did the school know about the bullying? Sometimes a teacher can tell if one of her students is acting a little different, perhaps becoming very quiet in class. The teacher needs to talk to that student, but maybe that didn't happen in this instance. Tyron?"

"The school doesn't know a lot of things that go on every day."

"I'm sure you're right, Tyron, and that's why both students and adults need to speak up."

"Why wasn't the gun locked up so the shooter couldn't use it? Did the mother of Bill get him help, or did she just tell the principal she did? We will never know the answer to these two questions. Why didn't the boy being bullied tell his parents or someone older? Charley"

"Maybe he wasn't used to talking to his parents, and so he thought he had to be the one to handle it."

"Hannah?"

"I talk to my parents all the time. It's so sad he couldn't do that."

"What have you learned from this story? Sam?"

"We need to talk to our parents more, be aware of what is going on around us, and not be afraid to speak up when we see things that are not right."

"Bingo! You are so right, and if we all do these things, including myself, maybe we can stop tragedies like this from happening again. Sometimes I have felt bad about not telling the principal, but even with the other teacher telling the principal, it did not change what happened. Now I look at certain things more closely than I did in the past. I am more aware of what is going on around me. Class, you are a wonderful group of young adults, and I am so proud of all of you. I hope the rest of your day is as insightful as this one has been."

CHAPTER 26

"I have written three words and their definitions on the board. Charley, would you like to read the first one?"

"*Pride*, meaning 'worth, pleased, self-respect, dignity, accomplishments.'"

"Brenda, read the next one."

"*Determination*, meaning 'a decision arrived at, concluded, settled, resolved, a great fairness in carrying out a purpose.'"

"Tyron, the last one please"

"*Resilience*, meaning 'spring back, cheerfulness, rebound.'"

"Copy these off the board because this will be your assignment to be finished and handed in by Friday. I want you to write about what *pride*, *determination*, and *resilience* mean for you personally and give an example of each from your own lives. Be honest with yourself.

"Do you have pride in yourself? Do you have determination and resilience? If you don't own these, I want you to tell why. Only then can you make changes. Always think, do your choices make you proud of yourself and make your family proud of you?"

CHAPTER 27

"Relax and open your minds to what I have to say today. Write this in your notebook: *You can't keep from making mistakes for the future if you don't know the past.* America was built on democracy and religious freedom. Our forefathers fought and died for the opportunity to create a free nation. The Constitution and Declaration of Independence were created as a guide for this country, but people will always misinterpret them for their own benefit. A free nation always needs to improve and make good changes for everyone. Some changes our nation made were giving women the right to vote and own property, and abolishing slavery, to name a few. People saw these wrongs and worked hard to change them.

"People will always try to destroy our freedoms, so beware. There are people in this country trying to destroy our freedom of religion by burning churches, trying to take God off our government buildings, public places, and in our pledges to God and country. People are trying to change our history by removing and destroying statues. The country is being divided by politics and hate rather than working with our leaders to make good changes for all people. Teen suicide is rising, and the divorce rate is very high. You don't try to block out past history—you study it and learn from it and work hard to change the wrongs for the betterment of all people.

"Years ago, I saw the prime minister of Russia Nikita Khrushchev on TV. He announced at a conference of the UN, 'Russia will not destroy America—America will destroy itself from within.' Many countries have said the same thing, so beware. There will always be people trying to change our freedoms.

"Eleanor Roosevelt wrote shortly before her 1962 death, 'The course of history is directed by the choices we make and our choices grow out of the ideas, the beliefs, the values, the dreams of the people. It is not so much the powerful leaders that determine our destiny as the much more powerful influence of the combined voice of the people themselves.' [Meacham, 'Leadership Fails,' *TIME*, 12 Nov. 2018 (p. 31).]

"You twenty-five students are responsible for your future, and you're responsible for America's future, so know your history well, stay current, and make good choices so you can create your own future. Stay involved in the democratic process so we don't lose these wonderful freedoms. Spend your time wisely because every second of your time is precious.

"When one is at a funeral, do friends eulogize about the deceased's bank accounts, his stereo system? Instead, they speak about his qualities like kindness, generosity, and love of family. Be aware of what you want to be remembered for. If you spend your time pursuing material things, you will not have time for the things that are truly fulfilling like time with family and good friends.

"This becomes more clear with age, but you have the choice to see its importance for yourself right now. When you want to know what you're like, look around at your closest friends and say to yourself, 'Am I nourishing friends or am I draining them? Are friends draining me? What are my motives, choices, or actions?'

"Here are some guidelines to live by: When something doesn't work out right and you feel you've wasted your time, money, and talents, a higher power may use your efforts in ways you will not begin to understand in this life. I believe that higher power is God, and I have been given the freedom in this country to make that statement. Even when you're tired and discouraged, stand strong. Work on both the smallest and biggest tasks. It doesn't matter whether it's service, study, or manual labor. What seems unpleasant at the time can open up a greater opportunity. What seems like waste to you might reap big results later.

"These are the strengths that make a person great—his or her integrity, strong work ethics, kindness, love of God, humility, generosity, and love. The choices are yours for what you want your life to be. As I said in the beginning, history is important, and I think, since you are all citizens of the United States, you need to remember and reread the Bill of Rights, the United States Constitution, and the Declaration of Independence.

"Here is an example of the wisdom in those documents. At the end of the Declaration of Independence, it says, 'And, for the support of this Declaration, with a firm reliance on the protection of divine Providence, we mutually pledge to each other our Lives, our Fortunes, and our sacred Honor.'

"When I was teaching in a grade school, a fifth grade teacher had her class memorize the Gettysburg Address and recite it to all the classes in the school. I was so impressed. Now I want to be impressed with your understanding and memorization of the address, especially that wonderful ending, where it says, 'That this nation under God shall have a new birth of freedom and that government of the people, by the people, for the people, shall not perish from the earth.'

"You have two weeks after your Christmas break to memorize the address and preform it together in class. Now I would like to end the day with a prayer General McArthur penned to his son, Arthur, while General McArthur was stationed in Australia acting as supreme commander of the Allied Forces in the Southwest Pacific area."

> Build me a son, O Lord, who will be strong enough to know when he is weak and brave enough to face himself when he is afraid; one who will be proud and unbending in honest defeat, and humble and gentle in victory.
>
> Build me a son whose wishes will not take the place of deeds; a son who will know Thee—and that to know himself is the foundation stone of knowledge.

Lead him, I pray, not in the path of ease and comfort, but under the stress and spur of difficulties and challenge. Here let him learn to stand up in the storm; here let him learn compassion for those who fail.

Build me a son whose heart will be clear, whose goal will be high; a son who will master himself before he seeks to master other men; one who will reach into the future, yet never forget the past.

And after all these things are his, add, I pray, enough of a sense of humor, so that he may always be serious, yet never take himself too seriously. Give him humility, so that he may always remember the simplicity of true greatness, the open mind of true wisdom, and the meekness of true strength.

Then I, his father will dare to whisper, "I have not lived in vain." [Franklin and Toney 2018, 93-94]

CHAPTER 28

"Today we are going to have a little history lesson to go along with yesterday's lesson. I'm sure you have heard people say that we must keep the separation of church and state because it's in the Constitution. Either they don't understand the wording of the Constitution or they have never read it. The First Amendment of the United States Constitution reads, 'Congress shall make no law respecting an establishment of religion, or prohibiting the free exercise thereof; or abridging the freedom of speech, or of the press; or the right of the people peaceably to assemble, and to petition the Government for a redress of grievances.'

"There are points I would like to share about the First Amendment: (1) the First Amendment applies to the states and forbids state action which would violate the rights of religion; (2) In many countries one religion has been made the official or 'established' religion and has been supported by the government and that congress is forbidden to set up or provide in any way for such an established church in the United States; and (3) congress cannot prohibit the free exercise of religion, but it could pass legislation against any group which practiced immorality as religion.

"Nowhere does the First Amendment say 'separation of church and state.' Abbey, what does it mean?"

"It means the United States will not establish and support one religion but does support freedom of religion."

"Tyron, what do you think?"

"Isn't this establishing a specific religion by the government with all its prayers, writings on the walls of the government buildings, using the word *god*?"

"Does anyone have an answer? Ethan."

"Yes, the government is not demanding you believe in a specific god or any god at all. You have the freedom to believe or not believe. Our government was established in part on this belief. Freedom of religion was why many people left England. In the United States, you have the choice to believe or not to believe—it's your choice."

"Well said Ethan, thank you. Aiden, would you turn on the overhead so we can see the Washington

Monument and the landscape of the four government buildings, thank you.

"I think now is a good time to talk about the Washington Monument in Washington, D.C. In Washington, D.C., no building can ever be of greater height than the Washington Monument. On the cap are displayed the Latin words *Laus Deo*—meaning, 'Praise be to God.' No one can see these words from the ground because they are on the top of the monument, about 555 feet high, facing skyward.

"Plans were made for the White House to be to the north, the Jefferson Memorial to the south, the Capital to the east, and the Lincoln Memorial to the west so that across the landscape it would form a perfect cross, which it does to this day.

"Within the monument itself are 898 steps and 50 landings. Some of the stones share a message. On the 12th landing is a prayer offered by the City of Baltimore. On the 20th is a memorial presented by Chinese Christians. On the 24th is a presentation made by Sunday school children from New York and Philadelphia quoting Proverbs 10:7, Luke 18:16, and Proverbs 22:6. When the cornerstone was laid on July 4, 1848, deposited within it were many items, including the Holy Bible. A replica of the top of the monument was on display behind glass so visitors could read the writings that were on the top cap. [Mikkelson, "Laus Deo and Washington Monument, Snopes, 2005]

"In 2007, a Pastor was leading a group through the monument, and he noticed that the replica had been moved so that you could not see or read the words *Laus Deo* and the meaning. Those words instead were flush against the wall. He wrote the National Park Service, stating, 'If the creators of the monument were so grateful for their Heavenly Father (God) that they inscribed praise specifically to Him alone on one side of the cap, shall we then show disrespect to them and God by covering it up? If the National Park Service is seeking to preserve such historic sites with integrity and dignity as their creators intended them to be understood, then it seems only right that a full disclosure and education of the capstone's inscription be known to the public inside the Monument...' [Unruh, "Park Services Restores 'God'-WDN,"WDN, 2007] The capstone has since been repositioned so that visitors will be able to read the engravings on all four sides. Thanks to this pastor, he made a choice to speak up and now people are able to read what has been written on the cap.

"Washington District of Columbia was named after George Washington and the Washington

Monument was built to honor him. The following is Washington's prayer for America, 'Almighty God, we make our earnest prayer that thou wilt keep the United States in Thy holy protection, that Thou wilt incline the hearts of the citizens to cultivate a spirit of subordination and obedience to government; and entertain a brotherly affection and love for one another and for their fellow citizens of the United States at large. And finally that Thou wilt most graciously be pleased to dispose us all to do justice, to love mercy, and to demean ourselves with that charity, humility, and pacific temper of mind which were the characteristics the Devine Author of our blessed religion, and without humble imitation of whose example in these things we can never hope to be a happy nation. Grant our supplication, we beseech Thee, through Jesus Christ our Lord. Amen.' [Mikkelson 2007]

"I hope this lesson has inspired you to think about what a great country we have and what our forefathers went through to create the freedoms we take for granted. Take time to learn the wealth of information that is available to everyone. Although I have not seen the monument, it is on my bucket list to do some day, and I hope it will be on your list also. There is great history in Washington, D.C."

CHAPTER 29

It is Saturday morning, and I'm able to sleep in. My husband left early this morning to meet friends for breakfast. My eyes close, and I feel myself falling back to sleep.

Suddenly I hear the phone ring and I really don't want to answer it, but it might be one of my children trying to get a hold of me so I pick up the phone. Its Shirley's voice on the phone, telling me her daughter Carol passed away early this morning and she was sure I would want to know.

I'm surprised and quietly tell her, "I'm so sorry."

We talk for a while, and then she says she has to make some more calls, so we hang up.

She, I, and friends knew this was going to happen; but it's still hard when it does. Carol had been through so many trials the last few years. She had a great job in New York and moved back home to take care of her mother when her mother had a bad fall causing partial blindness. Carol soon developed problems with her jaws and was finding it difficult to eat. She was operated on, replacing her TMJs with new joints. Since her mother could not drive, her mother's friends and I traded off driving Carol to her doctor and therapy appointments. At one of these appointments, Carol told me she never knew her grandparents, and so she wanted me to be hers. I was so honored.

She had a college degree but wanted a psychology degree. I told her I thought that was a great idea and she could take courses online while she was healing. Perhaps it would help her get her mind off the pain. She signed up.

As she was nearing graduation, she was offered a very good job; but the day of graduation, she had a stroke; and two weeks later, she had another one. Carol was slowly losing her strength and soon became bedridden. She was always such a positive person with a great outlook on life and a strong faith in God, even with all the setbacks she was going through. I visited her, and with each visit, I would notice it was more difficult for her to speak. But she never lost her sense of humor.

As I sit here recalling our visits and conversations, the tears start rolling down my face, and

I feel so disappointed with God for not answering my prayers to heal Carol. But I soon realize God has healed her and she is whole again with love, faith, and that radiant smile of hers. She is loved and is with God's angels, just where she would want to be. I finally wipe my tears and look to heaven, knowing there is another one in God's loving care, and I say to myself, "I'm glad I had the opportunity to know you, Carol, and you will be greatly missed, granddaughter."

CHAPTER 30

"Good morning, class. This is your last day of class until the third of January. I know you all are looking forward to your winter break. How many of you are going to be out of town over Christmas break? Ten. And how many will be celebrating with other relatives besides their immediate families? Oh, good. Most of the class. I know you all will enjoy the days with family, decorated homes, wonderful meals, and special gifts. All wonderful blessings that should never be taken for granted.

"I would like to read you an excerpt from President Truman's annual Christmas Eve address to the nation on December 24, 1949."

My fellow countrymen:

To each and all, a Merry Christmas.

Once more I have come out to Independence to celebrate Christmas with my family. We are back among friends and neighbors around our own fireside. Christmas is the great epic of home.

Our homecoming here on this Christmas Eve in familiar surroundings sanctified by family associations through the years—memories of joys and sorrows, of life and death—is typical of similar family gatherings all over the country.

The memories of most of us go back to childhood when we think of Christmas. After all, the first Christmas had its beginning in the coming of a Little Child. It remains a child's day, a day of childhood love and of childhood memories. That feeling of love has clung to this day down all the centuries from the first Christmas. There has clustered around Christmas Day the feeling of warmth, of kindness, of innocence, of love-the love of little children—the love for them—the love that was in the heart of the Little Child whose birthday it is.

Through that child love, there came to all mankind the love of a Divine Father and a Blessed Mother so that the love of the Holy Family could be shared by the whole human family. These are some of the thoughts that came to mind as I gave the signal to light our National Christmas Tree in the south grounds of the White House.

Sitting here in my own home, so like other homes all over America, I have been thinking about some families in once happy lands. We must not forget that there are thousands and thousands of families homeless, destitute, and torn with despair on this Christmas Eve. For them as for the Holy Family on the first

Christmas, there is no room in the inn. Among these families—broken with the tragedy of homelessness—are myriads of little children who have never known what it was to have a home or a country that they or their parents or their brothers and sisters could call their own.

Let us not on this Christmas, in our enjoyment of the abundance with which Providence has endowed us, forget those who, because of the cruelty of war, have no shelter—those multitudes for whom, in the phrase of historic irony, there is no room in the inn.

In this blessed season, let not blind passion darken our counsels. We shall not solve a moral question by dodging it. We can scarcely hope to have a full Christmas if we turn a deaf ear to the suffering of even the least of Christ's little ones.

Since returning home, I have been reading again in our family Bible some of the passages which foretold this night. It was that grand old seer Isaiah who prophesied in the Old Testament the sublime event which found fulfillment almost 2,000 years ago. Just as Isaiah foresaw the coming of Christ, so another battler for the Lord, St. Paul, summed up the law and the prophets in a glorification of love which he exalts even above both faith and hope.

We miss the spirit of Christmas if we consider the Incarnation as an indistinct and doubtful, far-off event unrelated to our present problems. We miss the purport of Christ's birth if we do not accept it as a living link which joins us together in spirit as children of the ever-living and true God. In love alone—the love of God and the love of man—will be found the solution of all the ills which afflict the world today. Slowly, sometimes painfully, but always with increasing purpose, emerges the great message of christianity: only with wisdom comes joy, and with greatness comes love.

In the spirit of the Christ Child—as little children with joy in our hearts and peace in our souls—let us, as a nation, dedicate ourselves anew to the love of our fellowmen. In such a dedication we shall find the message of the Child of Bethlehem, the real meaning of Christmas.

"As you are enjoying your holiday festivities, please remember those who are less fortunate. I would like all of you to write a letter of the changes you would wish for in this country and in the world, changes that would make people's lives better and changes for peace. How would you make this happen? I will look forward to reading the great changes you all would make. And remember, you all could make these changes happen in the future."

CHAPTER 31

It's Wednesday, and I'm headed home. There will be no school tomorrow due to Christmas break. We started celebrating Christmas the weekend before December 25, after our children began marrying and moving out of town. Our home was too small to house the entire family, but our wonderful neighbors came to the rescue. They gathered together and formed a plan to help house some of our children and their families during their stay. They will also help us by picking up some of the family members from the airport if needed. Where did these angels come from? I think my children enjoy seeing them as much as they do us.

Two of our children and their families will drive in from Kansas and Nebraska. They will arrive this Friday. My husband and I, with the help of "Grandpa Phil," as the kids call him, will drive to the airport Friday morning and pick up the rest of the family.

They will leave on Sunday after church. As everyone is packing up to leave, Grandpa Phil and Grandpa Jim will knock on the door with offers to drive people to the airport. Our children may have moved away, but we are blessed to have wonderful neighbors who still provide that sense of family. A few weeks later, we usually host a dinner party for our great neighbors. They and our family make our Christmas the most wonderful time of the year.

CHAPTER 32

I have spent my Monday writing letters to the parents of my students to let them know how proud I am of their son/daughter and how much he/she has contributed to the class. Thanks to their parenting, they have raised some wonderful teenagers who will be fine citizens of whom they can be very proud.

Now I'm ready to write to each student to let them know how proud I am of all their hard work in my class and what great people they are. I open my folder, and there at the top of the list is Jacob's name.

Jacob had a 4.0 GPA until last year when his grades dropped to Cs, with one B+. His father is a minister, and his mother is a secretary for the Royal Electric Company. He has two sisters and two brothers. I remember having his older brother in my Choices class, and he was a very good student.

Jacob likes music and history. He was in the glee club but then dropped out halfway through the year.

He participated in class until he showed up with a bruise on one cheek and a Band-Aid on his forehead. Recently, he has been saying "pass" whenever called upon in class. I know something is troubling him, and I hope I will be able to get him to let me know what is bothering him.

CHAPTER 33

"Welcome back, class, I hope you all enjoyed your winter break and made some good memories. I know I did. I had twenty-two people enjoying Christmas at my house with fun, laughter and good food. And they all arrived safely back to their homes, so many good blessings.

"Now it's time to get to work. Think back to yesterday or last week. You may have felt at times confused, dazed, muddled, bored, angry, resentful, doubtful, and apprehensive. Reflect upon those feelings you experienced. I want you to write about those feelings and explain why you think you had them.

"Was it because you had a fight with your family, you didn't get what you expected for Christmas, you had to visit relatives you weren't fond of, or your parents didn't give you permission to do the things you had planned to do over your break? What happened to make you feel that way? What do you think you could do to change your attitude about that experience? I also want you to write about how you feel when you're writing this assignment. You have the rest of the hour to complete this paper. Remember the word *honesty* when writing.

"Jacob, are you free after school today? I would like for you to come to my room because I need to talk to you."

"I have to pick up something from gym, but I'll be there."

I was preparing tomorrow's lesson when Jacob walked in.

"Mrs. Andrews, what did you want to talk to me about?"

"I noticed before Christmas break that you had some bruises and a cut on your forehead. Are you getting in fights at school?"

"No, I just hurt myself playing soccer."

"Jacob, are you being honest with me? You can share anything with me, and I will not share it with anyone else without your permission."

I could see Jacob thinking hard if he should tell me. All of a sudden, tears started forming in Jacob's eyes.

"Jacob what is it that's bothering you?"

"Mrs. Andrews, I'm gay, and I can't let my dad know. Some kids know, and we got in a fight. It's hard to be gay, and I wish I wasn't."

"Well, this is a hard subject. Thanks for being honest. I knew something had been bothering you."

This sure came as a surprise, and, Lord, I need your help NOW because I'm not an expert in this subject. I need to say the right things and be helpful to Jacob.

"Why do you feel you can't tell your dad?"

"He's a minister, and he would never understand and would probably throw me out of the house."

"I'm sure he would not do that, but I can understand why you don't want him to know. I will be honest with you. I don't agree with the lifestyle of the gay community and some of the demands they want, but I have compassion for them, and I love you, Jacob, no matter what or who you are, and I'm sure your dad feels the same way."

"He preaches about gays and how sinful they are, so I know he would not understand."

"Your dad needs to know. Would you like me to talk to him with you in the room here at school?"

"I don't know."

"It would be better if he learns it from you rather than hearing it from some friend or stranger."

"I guess you're right, but I'm not sure that my life will change for the better."

"It may not, but at some point, he has to be told."

Jacob hesitated and then said, "When do you want to talk to him?"

"How about Thursday after school in my classroom? I'll call him tonight."

About halfway through grading the papers that evening, I came to Hailey's paper. Hailey is smart, with a 3.85 GPA, has good answers, participates in nearly every discussion, and is quick to raise her hand even before you finish asking a question. She is a member of debate team but tends to speak out of turn in class and corrects other students during class discussions. Hailey is the oldest of six kids. Her dad works night shifts at the auto plant, and her mom works days as a court reporter. Even with so much going for her, sometimes I feel Hailey appears to feel insecure.

Hailey had written that one evening at dinner, she was discussing her plans to go to college with her parents. She has always dreamed of going to law school, but that evening, her father told her that he could not afford to pay for her to attend college, much less law school, and he did not have fond memories of lawyers after a crooked one tried to sue him. Hailey immediately started pointing out the reasons her father was wrong. She has been applying for scholarships and working weekends at McDonald's to help pay for college.

What started as a discussion of her dream turned into a shouting match with her parents. She couldn't fall asleep that night and felt like she was having a panic attack. She has been feeling angry and discouraged for the past week. She wrote that this assignment was making her even more angry and resentful of her father.

But as her paper continued, Hailey wrote that she also knew she had overreacted in her anger. By the end of the paper, Hailey realized that she needed to apologize to her parents for the outburst and try to talk to them in a more rational manner. She now realizes that she cannot force her parents to change the way they feel, but she can change how she responds to their criticism. "After all", Hailey wrote, "They are just concerned and want the best for me. I will not give up my dream of becoming a lawyer, but I understand it may take longer to do it on my own."

CHAPTER 34

"Good morning, class. Today I want you all to think of some positive feelings that you had during the break. Did anything happen that made you feel compassionate, grateful, gave you peace of mind, cheerful, or delighted? Focus on the people you interacted with. What kindness did you show them, what kindness did they show you, what made that day bright for you?

"Explain your good feelings and what made you feel that way. Sometimes it's the small pleasures that we tend to forget in our very rushed lives. I would like you all to complete this assignment by the end of the hour, and I will enjoy reading and grading them tonight."

I started grading papers as soon as school ended for the day. I usually wait until I get home but noticed the top paper was written by Brenda, and I couldn't help but start reading it.

Brenda struggles with school and has a 2.8 GPA. She finds algebra difficult but likes English class the best. She signed up for the Choices class because she heard that it requires a lot of writing, which is her strength. Brenda has an older sister with Down syndrome and heart problems, and her parents worry about her sister's future.

Brenda wrote about Christmas morning at her house. Her older sister, Claire, is twenty years old but functions at a much younger level. Brenda described the joy she felt watching her sister open presents, one in particular. Brenda's mother had spent weeks on a secret project.

When the sisters opened their gifts, they found matching scarfs and hats that their mother had knitted for them. Both girls were so excited that they put them on to model and ended up wearing them all day. Brenda went on to explain how her sister, Claire, is her best friend and how Claire's loving view of world has influenced Brenda's outlook in so many ways.

CHAPTER 35

"You all did a great job writing about your feelings the last two days. I was very impressed with your papers. I hope you don't mind that I shared some with my husband, but I was so impressed with your writing that I just had to brag about you. Don't worry, I didn't share any names.

"We all like to be around positive people. They make a day brighter, fun, and enjoyable. But we also know there will be days when we feel confused, doubtful, bored, resentful, or apprehensive. Those are days when we don't want to be positive. Have you learned any ways to rise above your negative feelings and act in a positive manner even when you don't feel like it? I am not trying to tell you that you should never have negative feelings or that the negative feelings are bad, but a positive person does not let them take over their lives.

"Your assignment today is to share how writing about your negative and positive feelings these past two days has made a difference in how you want to think and act. You can start writing now and I expect some good papers from all of you today."

The first paper I picked up to grade that evening was written by Zac. Zac lives in an upper-middle-class neighborhood with his mother who is a pediatrician. She adopted Zac when he was two months old and has been raising him as a single parent. Zac attended a private school through eighth grade but transferred to a public high school at the beginning of ninth grade. Zac is a good student with a 3.4 GPA and is the captain of the track team.

Based on his skin tone, I already know Zac is biracial, but I never realized how he felt about it until I started reading his paper. Zac wrote that he went to a private school, and every day he felt like he did not belong. That was the reason he begged his mother to let him transfer to a public school three years ago. He had been the only student of color at the private school and felt out of place and different than the rest of the students. He had thought that attending a public school would make him feel more comfortable.

Even though students at both schools accepted him and he was popular, he still came to school each day feeling like he was different. It wasn't that he was bothered by the fact that he was biracial; it was the fact that his birth mother had not wanted him and that he did not have a father. He knew without a doubt that his adoptive mother loved him and was his "real mother," but he could not shake the feeling of being rejected.

Because this assignment was about focusing on the gifts of kindness, Zac wrote that maybe it was time for him to focus on what was positive in his life instead of what was negative. He says he will try to focus on the fact that he has a lot of friends and an amazing mother who chose him to be her own son. He ended that paper saying that he knows the negative feelings will not disappear overnight, but he will try to stop concentrating on them and focus on the positive.

CHAPTER 36

"In your lifetime, you will find you have done things that should have been left undone. There will be things you've said that should have been left unsaid. You will act impulsively or speak without thinking. You will hurt people that you didn't mean to hurt. You will fail at times when you did not expect failure. You may knowingly or accidentally commit wrongs.

"This is part of life, just as positive actions are part of life. You have the opportunity to begin now by thinking before you speak and thinking before you act in such a way that these things will be only small wrongs on your plate once you are old. I want you to write a paper about some of the wrongs you have done and about how you would like to be able change them now. You have the rest of the hour to write this paper.

"Class, the hour is almost over. I will not be grading your papers. You are to save them and reflect on how you can change the way you respond to things or how you treat people. Whatever you have written on your paper, I know you will work on them and make good changes. You all are the best students. I know you will make good choices about changing the things that need change."

School is over, and I am waiting in my classroom with Jacob for his father to join us.

"Good afternoon, Pastor Clark, how nice of you to come. Please have a seat. Jacob has been dealing with a very hard subject. I had a talk with him and told him he needed talk to you. He was sure you would not understand, and I assured him that even if you did not understand, you both needed to talk about the subject.

"Jacob, please tell your Dad."

Poor Jacob was so nervous and was about to cry.

"Dad, I'm gay."

His dad was in shock!

"Jacob, you are not. Your mother and I raised you, and you're a Christian. What will this do to me as a minister? I'm against everything that gay people do and how they are sinners."

"Dad, I can't help what I am."

"Pastor Clark, I told Jacob I don't agree with the gay community, but I have compassion for them, and I love Jacob no matter what he is or does."

"That's easy for you to say. He's not your son."

"No, he's not, but I believe God loves all of us, no matter who or what we are. Jesus showed love for all mankind. He forgave sinners and I know He told them to sin no more, but that choice is up to the sinner. I feel there can be genetic and gene mistakes, and we have to learn how to handle them with love."

"I think the wrong one is a minister here. I'm not sure how I'm going to handle this, but I do love my son. Jacob, we need to go home and talk about this with your mother. Thank you, Mrs. Andrews, for bringing this to my attention."

"Thank you for taking the time to meet with me."

Lord, please be with this family and help them deal with this in a loving, tender way.

CHAPTER 37

"It's time to talk about what I call the 'big three'—Sex, Liquor, and Drugs. Each one could lead to addiction, risky behavior, and bad choices.

"I'm sure you have heard about our Supreme Court justice, Justice Kavanagh, who while in college was drinking beer and was accused many years later of attacking a girl at a party. If he hadn't changed his ways, he never would have become a Supreme Court justice. His wife and daughters had to go through hearing what he was accused of doing. They received horrible calls and felt the shame he went through. He could have been disbarred from practicing law. Be careful what choices you make while you're young.

"Girls, do you dress provocatively to get boys to look at you? Do you tease them, chase them, and drink at parties? I'm sure every boy would love that, but have you ever stopped to think about what could happen? Those boys' hormones are running wild, and when something bad happens to you girls, you call foul. Are you boys pressuring the girls, telling bad jokes, and going to wild parties where the beer and drinks are flowing? Have you ever stopped to think about what could happen?

"Recreational drugs can change your brain and affect thinking. Some parents probably couldn't get their child to take medicine for the flu when they were young, and now their child is damaging their bodies and brains with them. Hopefully, at birth, each of you were given a strong, healthy body, which is a gift that not everyone receives. It can be taken away by illness or accident.

"So why would anyone want to take a chance on messing it up? Some people take recreational drugs because their friends are taking them. That's a very poor reason. If your friends or group engage in behaviors you know are risky, you can speak up for them to make better choices. If you cannot affect a change in them, you can stand up for yourself and walk away.

"Sometimes this means leaving old friends behind and making new friends. True friends don't hurt their friends. They support them and want the best for them. I want the best life for each of you.

Your parents want the best life for you also, and you hurt them when you make poor choices.

"People often make excuses for teens by saying they're young and just experimenting. Hogwash, you are intelligent, great kids and have a good life ahead of you, so don't waste your future by doing things you can control. All of these things YOU, and only YOU, can control for yourself. There are many adventures to be had in life. Recreational drugs could be where your adventure begins and ends.

"Your assignment is to write a letter to a friend telling that person why he or she should stay clean. Please don't use real names. Explain why you want that person to be clean of sex, liquor, and drugs. You have about fifty minutes to finish."

CHAPTER 38

I was rushing from my social studies class to my Choices class when I saw Charley heading to class also. I stopped him and asked if he would come to my classroom after school today. I wanted to talk to him, and he agreed. He walked in while I was working on some papers.

"Charley, I'm glad you came. I wanted to tell you how happy I am that you are entering into class discussions. You are coming up with great answers. I wanted to know if things have improved for you at home."

"Well, sort of."

"Have you talked to your dad?"

"A little bit when he calls. But sometimes I just don't know what to say to him."

"That is a start. I want to tell you about a gentleman at my church. He's a divorce lawyer and also has a degree in counseling. He went through something similar to your experience when he was younger than you. Because of his experience, he decided to get a counseling degree as well as his law degree. Now he counsels kids with parents who are divorcing. He offers this help without charging a fee. I don't want to put you on the spot for an answer. However, think about it, and if you think it might help you, then with your permission, I'll talk to him. I can give you his phone number, and you can call him when you feel comfortable doing so."

I could see him thinking hard as to whether he really wanted this help.

"Well, I guess it wouldn't hurt."

"I think it could help a lot. He can help you talk to both your mom and dad and possibly ease some of the tension in your family. You're a good kid with a lot of weight on your shoulders right now. I am confident that you will find things will work out for the best, just give it more time."

"Thanks, Mrs. Andrews, you always seem to know the right things to say at the right time."

Chapter 39

I'm waiting for my husband to pick me up from school today. He dropped me off this morning because he wanted us to go out to dinner tonight. I asked him what the special occasion was, and he said every day was special and this one would just be more special. I really am married to a very sweet man. Now here he is, and as I get into the car, he gives me a sweet little kiss.

We are headed to the Top Light Inn downtown to eat. The inn has a revolving restaurant at the top with glass windows all around, giving us a wonderful view of the city below. I have some exciting news to tell him, but I am waiting until we are seated at the table before I share it with him.

After we ordered our food, Paul said, "I can tell you have something to tell me because you have that look of excitement on your face."

"I am excited," I tell him. "Do you remember me telling you about having my students in my Choices class recite the Gettysburg Address? When I walked into my classroom this morning, there were red, white, and blue streamers hanging from the ceiling, the lights, and just everywhere. The girls had red T-shirts on, and the boys were wearing blue T-shirts. They all wore eagle medallions on red, white, and blue ribbons around their necks, and each student was holding a star balloon.

"Jac was dressed as Pres. Abraham Lincoln standing at a podium that they must have borrowed from the auditorium. The music teacher Ms. Kindle, Dr. Sandiford, our principal Mr. Woodson, Sam's mother, Kaitlyn's mother, and Kathy's mother were there. Jac's mother had made red, white, and blue cupcakes for everyone to share. The students were lined up in front of the room, and they told me to have a seat on the chair in the middle of the room.

"Jac introduced himself as Pres. Abraham Lincoln and said that Lincoln delivered his Gettysburg Address in Pennsylvania on the battlefield where Civil War soldiers were buried. He gave his address on November 19, 1863. Lincoln had rewritten his speech five times, and while he was giving his address, he added the words 'under God,' and so it was changed to read 'that these dead shall not have died in vain, that this nation, under God, shall have a new birth of freedom.'

"After Jac's speech, the class recited the Gettysburg address beautifully, and then Ms. Kindle directed the students singing 'God Bless America.' Tears were streaming down my face, I was so moved. It was a very beautiful moment. Later I learned that the students had asked Ms. Kindle if she would help them with their singing. They all met her after school and had been practicing for the last two weeks.

"About ten of the students got together during Christmas break and came up with this idea. They called the rest of the students to let them in on their plan. The mothers of Nina and Hannah acquired the T-shirts and made the medals for each student with the help of their daughters. I told them they sure out-did the fifth graders in the grade school where I had worked.

"Mr. Woodson asked them if they would put on the same program for the opening of the assembly next week. I am so proud of them. To do something like this on their own makes them all so very special. So dinner tonight is just the icing on the cake and a wonderful way to end a very special day. Thank you, Paul."

CHAPTER 40

"I would like to congratulate you all on the wonderful program you put on yesterday. I'm still amazed at your ability to work together and put on such a beautiful program. Dr. Sandiford recorded it so that each one of you can have a copy. I will treasure my copy. I plan to show it to my whole family the next time we get together.

"You have put in an amazing amount of time planning and putting it on, and you all well deserve the A pluses you're getting. As you can see, I have put a treat on your desks so please enjoy. After that beautiful program yesterday, I wish that I had a different study planned for today. Let's try and get through it the best we can. When you have bad days, how do you feel? Let's list these feelings on the board. Who would like to go first? Shane?"

"Sometimes I'm toast and angry and I can't reason, much less listen."

Someone in the back of the room said *yes* to that comment.

"Anyone else? Nate?"

"When schoolwork piles up, I find myself in a bad mood, and I take it out on others."

"What does the bad mood cause you to do? Yell at people? Curse? Hide? Cry?"

"Yeah, I yell at people."

"Melinda?"

"I get so frustrated that I cry and throw things."

"Charley?"

"There are days when things have built up so much that I want to run away."

"Thank you for your comments. Sometimes life will be frustrating and one wants to run away and forget their problems. These problems could be complications of friendships, school, job, parents, and uncertainty about the future.

"Frustration can cause people to become weary and brokenhearted. They can become oversensitive and judgmental. That's when the pressure sets in, and we are battling thoughts and emotions. As you see by your classmates' answers, you are not the only ones having these feelings.

"When you are tired, your fears and doubts can multiply and your thoughts start spinning out of control, you feel discouraged, and loneliness can set in. You become vulnerable to bad decisions when you are unhappy. You need an attitude adjustment before things start spiraling out of control. Give me some things you can do to help you overcome these feelings."

There was a long silence, and then Abbey spoke up, saying, "I call a friend and we talk about those feelings, and before long, we both feel better and can see life is pretty good after all."

"Abbey, thank you for that answer. It is so important to talk to someone—a friend, a teacher, preacher, brother, sister, or parent. By talking things out with someone, you can identify your feelings, and it gives you a release from your thoughts. Life will always throw things your way that are hard to accept, but everyone must learn to overcome them and use them as a learning tool.

"You've heard the words 'We learn from our mistakes.' The tool for recovering from discouragement is to reach out to others. There are so many good people willing to listen, and sometimes you will be that person too. Everyone needs the skills to both seek and to offer help. I don't want to hear of any of you not using that tool. And remember, a good night's sleep is worth a whole lot of happiness."

CHAPTER 41

"Everyone, please clear your minds and reflect on what I'm going to say. Do you have a compulsion to be right, successful, or powerful? Do you have a confident spirit? And are you compassionate? Let us take each word separately.

"First word is *right*. Do you have the compulsion to always be right? When you're having a conversation with someone, do you always have to be right and have the last word? With this attitude, you miss out on so many different ideas and thoughts that other people have to share and you just might learn something from them. Learn to listen to the other side. You may be right, but they might be right also. Are you listening or trying to have the last word? Are you thinking of what you will say next, or are you intent on learning what the speaker has to say?"

"Second word is *successful*. If being successful means stepping on others, that's called greed. Being a successful person means how a person feels about themselves. Do you like yourself? Are you well thought of? Are your friends and family proud of you? Do you enjoy life? Each of these is a part of being successful."

"Third word is *powerful*. Are you in control of your emotions or do your emotions control you? Do you enjoy having control over your friends and family? A powerful person learns to have control over their emotions, their thoughts, and the things they do in life. They use that power for good."

"Do you have a confident spirit? Being confident does not mean being conceited by having an exaggerated opinion of one's ability or importance. It means you feel good about yourself and you care about yourself and about others. You're a trusted friend, and friends know they can trust you.

"I hope you all nurture a compassionate heart. I hope you care about your family, your friends, and those less fortunate. I hope you're willing to give help when needed and that you're concerned about doing the right thing."

"Now we come to the assignment for today. What kind of person are you? Use the words *right*, *successful, powerful,* and *compassionate* to tell about yourself. And as we all know, be honest when writing. That's the only way you can make changes in areas where you need change."

CHAPTER 42

"You may have heard of Captain Sully Sullenberger. I'd like to share this article about him with you."

On January 2009, he landed a plane on the Hudson River and saved himself, his crew and passengers. It has been called the "Miracle on the Hudson."

That day, shortly after taking off from New York City's LaGuardia Airport and on its way to Charlotte, N.C., Flight 1549 flew into a flock of geese and lost both engines. Sullenberger, the captain of the plane, said that in 42 years of flying with the U.S Air Force and as a commercial pilot, he'd never lost one engine-much less two. He said, he knew immediately, in a few seconds, how big a deal this was going to be. "I knew that this was going to be one of those events that divide one's life into before and after, and that was going to be true for everyone on the plane." After processing the situation, his voice calm and determined, Sullenbenger told the air traffic controller that their plane couldn't make it back to LaGuardia. They couldn't make it to any runway. Less than four minutes after taking off, they were bracing for impact on the Hudson River. Despite never having practiced a water landing, it simply wasn't possible with existing flight simulators. Sullenberger says he "was confident that he could take what he did know and adapt it and apply it in a new way to solve this novel event that we never anticipated or trained for. I didn't think I was going to die that day, but it was going to require every bit of knowledge, skill, experience and judgement I had attained over half a century to be able to do that."

And as most Americans know Sullenberger and his crew including First Officer Jeff Skiles did land that plane on the water without any casualties. And thanks to the rescue efforts of the ferries from NY Waterways, all 155 people on board made it back to land safely.

Sullenberger has since retired, written two books 'Making a Difference: Stories of Vision and Courage from American's Leaders.' And 'Sully: The Untold Story Behind the Miracle on the Hudson', which was made into a movie starring Tom Hanks. He's now a safety expert and speaker, and currently serves on the U.S. Department of Transportation's Advisory

Committee on Automation in Transportation. He still flies private planes because when you know at age 5 that you were born to do something, you can't just let it go. He speaks about safety and leadership in many industries, whether it's urging drivers to put away their cell phones or consulting on patient safety. He's an ambassador for human skills, showing moral courage, listening, respecting those who report to you, embracing empathy and willing to set aside your own interests for the common good. Sullenberger says that doing the right thing is often the harder choice, "it's really, ultimately, in your mind, about core values, about leadership and culture, creating an environment in which we are all willing and able to do our best work, that's really what sets apart the best from all the rest."

On basic civic duty, "I think it's critically important, especially when we get in a car, to have the sense of civic duty to remind ourselves that as citizens, there are things that we owe to each other. That we're really not islands unto ourselves and that if we didn't occasionally put our own immediate needs aside and delay our own gratification, if we didn't give these little gifts of civic behavior to each other, civilization wouldn't be possible." [Elbert, "America's Pilot", 2018]

"I would like you all to write down what lessons and ideas you have learned from Captain Sullenberger. I think he's a great role model for both the young and the old. I would encourage you all to see the movie. There are not many movies made that are emotionally uplifting and have people of personal character with happy endings that make you feel glad you took the time to watch. I think your time will be well spent."

CHAPTER 43

"I was so impressed with a story I read in Time magazine last month, and I thought it would be a great idea if I shared it with this class. It's about Simone Askew, the first black woman to lead the Corps of Cadets at West Point. The article reads in her words:

> "Coming into the Military Academy, where the ratio is about 80% men to 20% women, didn't have a huge impact at first. I was blessed to have great mentors who really encouraged and empowered me. But now I see how the imbalance affects the dynamics not only between men and women at the academy but also between the women here. Because we're such a small minority, there is a sense

of having to compensate for what people might think is an inherent weakness or deficit. I need to be on the top of my game. That feeling of being acutely aware of my gender is most apparent when I receive criticism from people who don't know me. You have to wonder, if they have no idea who I am and have never met me to assess my weaknesses or my strengths, why are they so angry about my achievements? But I never saw my race or gender as a roadblock to me being selected or even for me being competitive as a candidate. I resolved in elementary school that if someone didn't like me because of things I couldn't change, then that was their problem. I wasn't chosen to be first. I was chosen to be the First Captain." Askew, now is a Rhodes Scholar, graduated from West Point in May 2018. [Matalon, "Person of the Year," 2018]

"Captain Askew is such an impressive person. Her parents did a great job raising her, and she has given us so many wonderful lessons in this article. Chi, will you turn on the overhead? Now you can read this article on the blackboard. What are some of the lessons she describes that we have been learning or need to learn? Charley?"

"We had a lesson on getting to know a person before forming an opinion of what that person is like."

"Annie?"

"If you have pride in yourself, you will be able to stand up for yourself."

"Hailey?"

"She says, 'I never saw my race or gender as a roadblock.' I think she saw herself as a human being, and saw other people the same way, a person that embraced all people no matter who they were."

"Susan?"

"She has the strength and the willingness to accomplish her goals. She had pride in herself."

"Nina?"

"She said she had good mentors. I'm sure she meant teachers and parents, but maybe she meant friends also. Our lesson on 'you are known by the friends you keep and friends who want the best for you.' That had a good impression on me, and I think that's the way Simone might have felt."

"Good thinking, class, you always come up with great comments."

CHAPTER 44

"Sam, would you please pass out these papers for me? When Sam is finished, I would like you all to follow along while I read these ideas you can practice every day to help others and improve your character. Some of these ideas are not new, we have talked about them before, but it doesn't hurt to hear them again.

"We all need compassion for others who are different than us either by religion or race; compassion for the hurting and war-torn countries; and compassion for the poor, the disadvantaged, and the lonely. We can all use compassion to make this a better world to live in. When you have kindness in your own hearts, you are able to pass that kindness on to others.

"Practice compassion at home. Help your brother or sister with homework, help them with learning a new game, or if they've had a bad day, listen and learn how to make their day brighter. Do you listen to your parents and try to please them by helping out at home? Most people feel good about themselves when they are helping others and by helping others you're letting them know you care.

"When we listen to what others are saying, we're showing them love and respect. We need to listen to teachers, friends, and family. Listen to what is being said—you just might learn something new. Learn to be a good listener. Learn to forgive one another. When we hold hate in our hearts, it only hurts ourselves.

"Be a better person—forgive and release that hurt. Let 'forgive and forget' be your motto. Reach out with hugs, smiles, and encouraging words. People need to stop being self-focused and show they care about others and those that are different than them. You have an opportunity to change the world around you. You can make a difference in this world, and you have to decide what kind of world you want to live in.

"Exercising is so very important. It can help to prevent depression. So get that body moving in sports, walking with friends, running, or doing yoga. Enjoy the outdoors with fun activities, and be active. Get involved with different groups, clubs, politics, learn from each other, read different books, talk to people with great ideas, share your ideas with others. Make a difference in your world.

"Practice replacing negative thoughts with positive ones. Do this daily, and you will find you will become a much happier person. Positive thoughts make you feel good about yourself and others.

"Now each day, choose one of these to practice, and you will find that you will become much happier and a very interesting person to know."

CHAPTER 45

"Today at lunch, you are to sit with someone that is eating alone or someone who you think is being treated poorly. This is your assignment for this week. You are to get to know them, befriend them, and be able to tell some of their history. But please don't gang up on one person. There are at least 620 seniors at this school, and I'm sure there are many students that need a little kindness thrown their way. If you do this the right way, you might enjoy making a new friend and brighten someone else's life.

"We all tend to form our own little groups of people that we do things with and forget that there are other people that want to belong, feel left out, or feel discouraged and alone. Those are the people in life that need someone like you to just care. They need someone to greet them at school with a 'Hi, how are you?' When someone says that to you, how does that make you feel? Warm inside, someone cares about me? There are small things we all can do to make someone's day brighter. Sometimes, just a smile or small words of encouragement help. I think doing these small things will even make your day brighter, knowing you put a smile on someone's day.

"I would like for you to do this every day for at least a week and hopefully longer. I don't want you to use names on your paper, but I want at least five paragraphs describing how this made you feel and how you think the other person might have enjoyed the attention. I hope this will not be a onetime thing for all of you but that it will become a way of life, befriending those you don't know and those who just need someone to care. I know you all can do this and do it well because through all the assignments I have given you, the one thing that stands out is that each of you has a very caring heart.

"When my parents passed away and we were cleaning out their house, I came across a book of poems called *A Heap O' Livin'* by Edgar A. Guest, written in 1916. This book was reprinted thirteen times in three years. One of the poems in this book is called 'Be a Friend.'"

> Be a friend. You don't need money
> Just a disposition sunny;
> Just a wish to help another
> Get along some way or other;
> Just a kindly hand extended
> Out to one who's unbefriended;
> Just the will to give or lend,
> This will make you someone's friend.
>
> Be a friend. You don't need glory.
> Friendship is a simple story.
> Pass by trifling errors blindly,
> Gaze on honest effort kindly,
> Cheer the youth who's bravely trying,
> Pity him who's sadly sighing;
> Just a little labor spend
> On the duties of a friend.
>
> Be a friend. The pay is bigger
> (Through not written by a figure)
> Than is earned by people clever
> In what's merely Self-endeavor.
> You'll have friends instead of neighbors

For the profits of your labors;
You'll be richer in the end
Than a prince, if you're a friend. *WOW!*

"Now you all can use the rest of the hour to catch up on any homework you haven't finished from your other classes or read."

CHAPTER 46

"I hope sitting with someone different at lunch last week was a good experience for each of you. Don't use names but tell the class about your kindness shown to someone else and how they responded to you. Who would like to go first? Kaitlyn?"

"I sat with a girl who was alone at the back of the lunchroom. She was not real clean and had on some very old clothes with a stain on her shirt and pants, and her hair looked like it hadn't been washed in a while. I started by telling her my name and asked hers. I could see she wondered why I had sat down with her, but as we started talking, she let me know that she was kind of an outcast at this school.

"She slowly explained that she and her family had to move to a shelter when their house burned down last year and had not been able to get back on their feet. She was ashamed of the clothes she had to wear, and because of all the people in the shelter, it was hard to find a time to use the shower and bathroom. I was starting to feel real sorry for her, and when I went home, I asked my mom if it would be okay if I gave her some of my cloths that I hadn't worn in a long time.

"My mom also bought some shampoo that you don't have to use water with, some bars of soap, and some towels and wash clothes. I hid them in a bag with a zipper so no one would know what was inside and gave it to her after school. Well, she started crying, gave me a hug, and couldn't stop thanking me. I just can't explain how good I felt inside, and I will still be eating with her and hope my friends will do the same. When she came to school yesterday, she looked like a new person wearing a smile across her face."

"Kaitlyn, I am so proud of you, what a very beautiful story. Who else would like to share their experience? Jacob?"

"I decided to sit with a kid that had been having trouble in school with his grades and sat alone most of the time. I also started by telling him my name, and he asked why I was sitting with him. That surprised me, and I wasn't sure what to say next so I just asked him to tell me his name, which I should have really known.

"He had a little stutter to his voice, but after we talked a little while, I got used to it. He said he really didn't like school and had a hard time with his classes. I asked if I could help him after school with some of his work, and he asked, 'Why do you want to do that?' Well, there I was, taken back again with his response, so I said I had had a hard time with my classes at first, and so my mom got me help and now I am really pretty good in all my classes. I told him to think about it overnight and let me know the next day.

"When I sat with him the next day, he still was wondering why I would want to help him, and I said, 'Sometimes we all need a little help in life.' He said, 'I'll meet you after school and let you know if I want your help.' I met him after school, and we worked on his chemistry. After I explained what he seemed to have missed in the first days of class, he was able to understand a little better. I told him I would be able to help him a couple of times a week if he needed it.

"He slowly became more friendly, and I have to say, I was starting to kind of like him, and it made me feel good to be able to help him. Last week he shared a big piece of cake his mother had made, and boy was that good."

"Two wonderful stories from two great students."

We continued on the rest of the hour, and I don't know who enjoyed the stories more—me or the class. I hope they all remember this assignment and how good it made them feel to help others.

CHAPTER 47

"Last week you made friends with someone at lunch that you really hadn't known before and I shared a poem with you about friendship. I want you to write a paper on what friendship means to you and how you might continue that friendship every day. Explain what makes a friendship special, long lasting, caring, and kind. You have the rest of the hour to complete the assignment."

After I dismissed everyone, I noticed Kaitlyn was not hurrying out of class like she usually does. She was waiting 'til everyone else left. Kaitlyn is a good student with a 4.0 GPA, very pretty, a cheerleader, but stays within her own group of friends. Her mother is a pediatrician and her dad is a lawyer for a well-known firm in town. She has one brother who plays football. The whole family is very active in church, and she and her brother both sing in the youth choir. Her parents said she plans to go to college and follow in their footsteps and may combine a degree in both medicine and law. I'm sure she will be very successful in whatever she does.

"Kaitlyn, can I help you?" I asked.

"Mrs. Andrews, I would like to share something with you. You're always telling us to be honest with ourselves and others. Well, I signed up for this class because I thought it would be another easy class that I could make an A in. I didn't expect it to change my thinking.

"Last night I was watching the news on TV, and they had a segment on homeless people, and I found myself feeling so much compassion for them. I never would have thought anything about it several months ago, but having spent three weeks with the different charities and you asking us to eat with someone at lunch that might just need someone to care about them made me realize how very self-centered my life has been.

"School has always been easy for me, and I run around with kids who think the same as I do, and I guess I kind of looked down on others who were different. This class has changed all that and I just wanted you to know."

"Oh, Kaitlyn, you have made my day. My hope has always been that what I teach would change lives, and your story is so precious. I will treasure it in my heart. Thank you so much for sharing it with me."

I gave Kaitlyn a hug. I know this was hard for her to tell me, but I'm so proud of her for realizing she needed to change.

CHAPTER 48

"By now, you should have a pretty good idea about making good choices. Today I want you all to write a paper on making those good choices and what you plan to accomplish in ten years. For your homework tonight, type your paper, print it, and add your picture on the right-hand side. Please get started so you will finish by the end of class. Now don't forget the photograph of yourself on the finished paper."

CHAPTER 49

I've read all their papers they handed in yesterday and have given them a grade. These students have written wonderful papers on what they hope to become in the future, and I know each one will succeed. What a great year this has been.

CHAPTER 50

"I'd like to introduce Superintendent Dr. Sandiford. He is a good friend and mentor and the one I persuaded to give me this class fifteen years ago.

"You all will be graduating in the next couple of days, and as you can see, I have invited seven of my former students to join us today. I will start from the left and introduce them to you. Dr. Hailey Cosmo is head of the heart department at Jersey Springs Hospital. She graduated in 2003.

"Next is Dr. Susan Volt. She started a wonderful origination called Mary's Loving Hands for abandoned and unwanted babies. She graduated in 2004.

"Next is Sally Mathew, who is the CEO of a company she started called Grow Strong. They make baby formula for foreign starved countries. She graduated in 2006.

"Next is Fire Chief John Murdock, fighting fires here in our very own city, who graduated in 2006.

Next is Police Chief Roger Hahn from Kansas City, graduated in 2007. Next is Lieutenant Charles Day of the Navy, graduated in 2005.

"And Susan Jones who founded the Song and Dance Studio in the inner city for underprivileged kids. She graduated in 2008. Charley Burger started a company and is CEO of Get a Grip. They make metal hooks for camping, the Army, and the Navy Seals. He also graduated in 2005.

"Tyron Johnson, who formed a company called Hang Tight to find jobs for people who have been on welfare, graduated in 2007. And last but not least is Jerome Smith who started a much-needed heart surgery department in Salisbury, Rhodesia, Africa, graduated in 2003.

"They will be handing out books that I have made from the papers you wrote last week about good choices and about what you hope to become in ten years. In the back of these books, you will find the writings of all of these former students, what they wrote about themselves back when they were seniors. They have also added the things they accomplished since they graduated.

"I hope these stories will be an inspiration to all of you. I have great hopes for every one of you. You are all capable of doing great things. Please come up and receive your books of Choices. After all of the books have been handed out, please feel free to talk to each of these wonderful people who have given their time today to meet with all of you."

CHAPTER 51

As I walked into my class today, there was Dr. Sandiford, Mr. Woodson, and all my students. This will be my last class of the year, and I am really going to miss teaching.

"Mr. Sanford and Mr. Woodson, how nice to see you both visiting our class today."

Dr. Sanford said, "Mrs. Andrews, would you come and stand by me? I think your class has something to tell you."

Kaitlyn stood up with something large in her hand and said, "Mrs. Andrews I would like to present you with 'The Declaration of Truth, Honesty, and Confidence.' It reads,

> The students of Mrs. Andrews'
> class have been taught what
> makes a person liked, honorable,
> and a blessing to society by shar-

ing her honesty, her kindness, and caring about each one of her students. We dedicate this day, May, 27th, 2019, as a day to be celebrated each year here at Kirk Hill High School to honor her way that makes learning a lifestyle and a credit to our nation.

"We have all signed our names below, including Dr. Sanford and Mr. Woodson."

My tears really started flowing, and I had a hard time talking.

"Today and every day, you all have made me so proud of each and every one of you. You have made yourselves proud human beings by your knowledge, hard work ethic, and your great sense of humor. I expect great things from all of you. You have been a great joy in my life. Thank you so much for the honor you have given me today, and I expect to see all your names in the paper in the future with the words 'The best and greatest class Kirk Hill High School has ever produced.' Now let's dig into those pizzas in the back of the room, and we would like Dr. Sanford and Mr. Woodson to join us."

The students were wonderful and were enjoying telling some of the funny stories that happened in this classroom, and I could see Dr. Sanford and Mr. Woodson enjoying them also.

"Well, class, it's time to end our wonderful time together, and as you know, I will miss each and every one of you. I want Zac to hand out your grades. Don't open them until I say 'Go.'"

As the last grade was handed out, I yelled, "Go!" and a cheer went up from the class that I'm sure was heard all over the school.

"Each and every one of you great students earned an A in this class and kept the class A record going. Thank you!"

The hour was up, and it was time for the school year to end.

"I have an envelope with a note in it to give you as you leave, and I hope you will use it as a bookmark in the future. Enjoy your summer, and if you ever need someone to talk to, you know how to get a hold of me. I send my love and gratitude with each one of you."

As they left, I gave them each the note and a big hug.

The note read,

> You are very special, and your
> choices tell who you are, to your-
> self, your parents, to others and
> to your creator God and his son
> Jesus Christ. Know you are loved.
> Mrs. Andrews.

P.S. May your choices always be good ones.

Sources

"Declaration of Independence." In *World Book Encyclopedia*, 67, 1968.

Elbert, Sarah. "America's Pilot", Renew by United Healthcare-Fall 2018, pp. 12–15

"Gettysburg Address." In *World Book Encyclopedia*, 164, 1968.

Graham, Franklin and Donna Lee Toney (2018). *Through My Father's Eyes*. Thomas Nelson, 2018.

Guest, Edgar A. *A Heap O' Livin'*. Chicago, IL: The Reilly & Lee Co., 1916, p 97.

Matalon, Molly. "Person of the Year." Time, March 1, 2018.

Meacham, Jon. "Leadership Fails." *Time*, November 12, 2018, p 31.

Mikkelson, David. "Laus Deo and Washington Monument" Snopes.com, January 25, 2005.

Accessed June 14, 2019. www.snopes.com/fact-check/washington-monument.

Peters, Gerard, and John T. Woolley. "Harry S. Truman, Address in Connection with Lighting of the National Community Christmas Tree on the White House Grounds." The American Presidency Project. UC Santa Barbara. Accessed June 14, 2019. https://www.presidency.ucsb.edu/node/229849.

"The United States Constitution." In *World Book Encyclopedia*, 141, 1968.

Unruh, Bob. "Park Service Restores 'God'—WDN." WDN, October 30, 2007. Accessed June 14, 2019. www.wnd.com/2007/10/44289.

ABOUT THE AUTHOR

Marilyn Guier grew up in Webster Groves, Missouri, where she always felt safe. Her brother, sister, and she were raised in a Christian home where Sundays were spent attending church and having family time together. Her parents never preached to them, instead showed their Christian belief in their kindness to others and daily living.

She went to college to get a teaching degree but married after two years and now has five wonderful children and eight delightful grandchildren. She worked as a teacher's aide for the Special School District and then for the Parkway School District in St. Louis County. When she retired, she volunteered for the Oasis Program, helping children learn to read. She enjoys traveling with her family, making greeting cards for family and friends, and working in her yard and garden.